I Am Pan:

The Fabled Journal of Peter Pan

by Boyd Brent

Author contact: boyd.brent1@gmail.com

Copyright Boyd Brent

The right of Boyd Brent to be identified as the Author of the work has been asserted by him in accordance with the Copyright, Designs and Patents act of 1988.

This novel is a work of fiction. The characters and their names are the creation of the Author's imagination and any resemblance to actual persons, living or dead, is entirely coincidental.

I Am Pan

One day, someone from the real world called J.M. Barrie is going to write my life story. Tiger Lily is certain of it. She said she saw him in a dream, hunched over a desk and scribbling things about me. "He isn't even going to hear about you first-hand from someone who *actually* knows you, Peter. But *fourteenth*-hand from someone who's heard about you in the vaguest of terms."

"How vague, exactly?" I asked her.

Tiger Lily peered at my ears. "Pointy-ears vague. Is that vague enough for you?"

I scratched at my ear, which is perfectly round. "I see," I said. "And?"

"And how accurate can his book be?"

I placed my fisted hands on my hips. "Well, let him write it! And knock himself out if he wishes." And by that I did not mean he should punch himself in his own head until he loses consciousness; I meant let him do his worst and write whatever he likes.

Tiger Lily sat down on a rock and sighed. "But you're a real hero, Peter. You owe it to the world outside the Neverland to

3

tell them the *truth*."

I drew my sword and lunged at an imaginary pirate. "What would you have me do?"

"Find this J.M. Barrie."

"Why?"

"How else are you to challenge him to a duel for making up stories about you?"

I froze mid-lunge and narrowed my eyes at her. "Is J.M. Barrie a *pirate*?"

"No, Peter. He's an author."

I slid my sword back into my belt. "I can't go around challenging authors to duels."

"Why ever not?"

"It doesn't sound very heroic."

Tiger Lily adjusted her Indian headdress. "Oh, I know! Why don't you keep a journal? That way you can tell your tales of derring-do the way they actually occurred." If you have my journal in your possession, I must have liked her suggestion.

Journal entry no. 1

I flew beyond the Neverland today, to a place in the real world called London – a great city where grown-ups rush about like headless chickens trying to earn a crust. And by *crust* I don't mean pies without filling. It is money they seek, to pay things called *bills*, and to buy things to impress others – those who live next door, mostly. It's not all dreadful in the real world, though, because children live there. I watch them at play, and marvel at how they use their imaginations to escape it. I try my best not to think about how they're morphing into grown-ups. It makes me break out in a cold sweat whenever I do. You may think that I too must grow up one day. Think again! I promised myself long ago that I would never allow myself to morph into a man who chases a crust by day, and allows his imagination to wither by night.

I have a secret to tell. Come closer now, and I will whisper it: there is one family in particular I like to watch. They are called the Darlings – a family of two grown-ups and three children. The children are called Wendy, John and Michael. They live in a grand red-brick house on a street lined with tall oak trees. I was attracted to their bedroom window by the glow of their night lights. Did I mention that I can fly? I can, and without the aid of wings or a motor. If not for this ability, I would never be able to leave the Neverland, which is located amongst the stars. We have no space programme here – at least none that I am aware of, although, I would put nothing past James Hook in his quest to plunder worlds beyond our own. But more of Hook later.

When I first looked through the window into the bedroom of the Darling children, I beheld a room with lime-green walls and lush red carpet. I saw three beds, each with its own night light. In the middle of the room was a doll's house big enough for a child to shelter in. I visited their window regularly, and realised their parents were creatures of habit. After their father kissed them goodnight, their mother would read them stories until they fell asleep. I always arrived in time to watch their mother read to them. Tiger Lily said that makes me a Peeping Peter, but Tinker Bell told her that there is no such thing as a Peeping Peter. "Peter is a Peeping *Tom,*" she said. Tiger Lily placed an arrow in her bow, took aim at her, and told her to admit she was wrong. Tinker Bell waved her wand and said she would not. I thought it best to change the subject before they came to spells and arrows. "I sometimes wonder," I said, "what it would be like to have someone kiss you goodnight every night, like those Darling children have." My question seemed to cheer Tink and Tiger Lily. They cast aside their weapons and said I should choose one or other of them to conduct an experiment. "What kind of an experiment?" I asked suspiciously.

"A goodnight kiss experiment," they replied. I said I would need time to think about that, and flew quickly away.

Once again, I have interrupted my own train of thought. And so back to the Darling house…

Yesterday, after their mother had finished reading to them, she opened their bedroom window. I hovered below it, pressed my body against the brickwork, and waited until the coast was clear. Once I was certain that they were asleep, I flew in through the window and landed on the carpet in my bare feet. The carpet was as lush as a bed of dandelions in spring, and so I spent some time pinching it with my toes. As I picked the fluff from between my toes, I hovered from bed to bed and took a closer look at the children. When I told Tink what I'd done, she clasped her cheeks in horror, and told me I was worse than a Peeping Tom now. "In the real world they call what you did *breaking and entering*. And they lock people up who do it!"

"Calm yourself, fairy! They wouldn't lock me up. I didn't break anything."

"It doesn't matter. You entered and that's just as bad," said Tink.

"Of course I did. How else was I to get a closer look at the children?"

Tink sighed. "If you *should* end up in court before a judge, accused of breaking and entering, it might be best if you didn't make that your defence."

"We have no courts in the Neverland, Tink."

"Lucky for you. What's so interesting about this *Darling* family, anyhow?" she asked.

"They make me wonder…"

"About what?"

"Do you think I ever had parents that kissed me goodnight?"

"Don't you remember?"

I shook my head. Tink sat beside me and placed a hand on my shoulder. "Are you sad, Peter?" she asked. "Only I don't think I could stand it if you were."

I stood up, placed my fisted hands on my hips, and turned to face her. "You imagine that great heroes have time for sadness?"

"Your modesty knows no beginnings, Peter," she said.

"You imagine you will win me over with flattery?"

"You think that *flattery*?"

"Hush now and let me explain: I have decided to make some friends in the real world."

"Friends with who?"

"The Darlings, who else?"

"What are they like?"

"Who could say? Wendy, Michael and John were all sleeping soundly."

Tink sprouted her silver wings and fluttered up into the air. I looked up at her. "How do you know their names?" she asked.

"They are carved into the wooden headrests of their beds."

"Are they horribly spoilt, then?"

"Maybe so. But I shan't know until I meet them."

Tiger Lily had been hiding on the branch of a tree above, and now she made herself known. "Isn't it forbidden even to *talk* to anyone in the real world?"

"Forbidden? By who?" I said, drawing my sword.

"Hook, I believe," said Tiger Lily, placing an arrow in her bow and casting her gaze about for pirates.

I laughed. "Since when did we take orders from James Hook?"

"Since never!" said Tiger Lily, letting an arrow fly into the night.

"Both of you listen," I said. "Hook only makes such rules because he cannot reach the real world himself."

At that moment, the sun's first rays peeked over the mountains to the east, and the first cock began to crow. "It's time to find them, Peter," said Tink.

I left Tink and Tiger Lily, and flew to the Lost and Found Lagoon to find the Lost Boys. They rely on me to find them every morning, and only then can their day begin. Finding them is not so difficult, as they've taken to losing themselves in the same place every night. I flew down and landed on the usual rock, folded my arms, and cleared my throat. "I hereby declare the Lost Boys to be found."

"What time do you call *this*?" asked Nibs, looking up at me.

"I thought the right time. Did the first cock not just crow?"

Tootles got up and stretched. "No, it didn't. The first cock has probably forgotten it crowed. What have you got to say to that?" he asked.

"That I must have got lost in my imagination, and time passes so quickly there. Although, cocks aren't best known for their excellent memories," I said.

"Peter's not wrong," said Slightly. "I talked at length to a cock once, and it had precisely nothing to say for itself. I got the impression it couldn't remember a single thing, not even when I asked it what it did in the two seconds before I arrived."

Nibs shook his head. "What did you expect from a cock? All they remember is how to walk, peck and crow."

"I'm starved," said Nibs, reaching for his fishing rod.

At the edge of the lagoon Slightly, Nibs and Tootles cast their fishing lines. You may be wondering about the other Lost Boys. If so, then wonder no more. There are only three, but that's not to say we're not on the look-out for new Lost Boys – although finding new Lost Boys is as hard as finding a cat in a dog pound. I flew up onto the precipice above them, and shielded my eyes from the sunlight that glinted off the water.

"It's still there?" asked Nibs.

"Yes," I said.

Nibs cast his line. "What's it doing?"

"It's floating. What else would a pirate ship be doing in a harbour?"

"And just to confirm: it's not floating in our direction?" said Slightly.

"Relax. Its sails are down. And so too is its anchor."

"So why were you late this morning, Peter?" asked Tootles.

"I visited the real world last night."

"Again?" said Nibs.

"That's right, and it's a long way away."

"The further the better, if you ask me," said Tootles.

I crouched down and picked at some moss on the rock. "It isn't all bad in the real world," I said.

"It must be nearly all bad if it's full of grown-ups," said Nibs.

"It's true: the grown-ups have allowed their imaginations to wither." At this terrible truth the Lost Boys shuddered.

Slightly skimmed a stone across the water in the direction of the pirate ship. "Even pirates haven't allowed that to happen."

"Why *do* you keep going back there, Peter?" asked Tootles.

"To see the children, of course."

Tootles pulled at his braces, which grow tighter by the day. "But why?" he asked.

"Because they are turning into grown-ups, and I fear for their imaginations."

"Not a lot you can do for the imaginations of children in the real world," said Nibs.

"Maybe I can't help them *all,* but…"

"But what, Peter?" asked Tootles.

"But the *Darlings*," I murmured.

The Lost Boys looked one to the other and sniggered. Between sniggers, Slightly said, "While it may be that the children of the real world are *darlings*, perhaps you shouldn't refer to them as such."

"No," chuckled Tootles, "not unless you want to grow pigtails."

I stamped my foot. "Silence! Do you imagine that I, Peter Pan, am going soft?"

"No. Of course not," said Nibs, shoving the other two.

"*Darling* is the name of a family. Two parents called Mr and Mrs Darling, and three children called Wendy Darling, John Darling, and Michael Darling."

"That's an awful lot of *darlings*," said Tootles, and all three fell about laughing.

I stood up straight and filled my chest with air. "Grow up!" I said.

My ill-thought-out instruction brought looks of horror to their faces. Nibs, who had turned slightly redder in the face than the others, said, "Did you just tell us to *grow up*?" He grabbed his heart as though to prevent it from bursting.

"Too cruel," said a horrified Slightly.

"Take it back, Peter! Or it might come true!" cried all three.

I reached up and grabbed three imaginary backs from the air. I took a fourth for good measure, then apologised for the worst instruction any young person can give another. Nibs worked at calming his breathing. "You're spending *much* too much time in the real world, Peter."

"It can't be helped. The Darlings need my help."

"To do what?"

"To prevent the loss of their imaginations."

"Does that mean you're going back to see them again?"

"Oh, yes. Tonight."

Journal entry no. 3

That night when I arrived at the Darlings's house, I was pleased to find the window open again. I shot high over the house and looked across the rooftops to the clock tower called Big Ben. It was midnight, and I felt certain they would be sleeping by now.

I flew through the open window and landed on the carpet. I turned and looked back out of the window at the full moon. And because I know *how* to look, I watched the moon-fairies that fly across it on the hour. This particular hour meant there should have been twelve, but I counted thirteen, and made a mental note to stop and shake a finger at them on my way home. Barely had I made this note, when I felt a tap upon my shoulder. I turned quickly, and looked into the face of the youngest of the Darling children, Michael. Michael has a shock of blond hair, and high and rounded cheekbones like those of a cherub. "I was hoping you'd come back," he said, rubbing his eyes.

"You *were*? But why?"

"So you can teach me," he whispered.

I motioned to the window behind me. "Teach you how to count the fairies that float across the moon every hour?"

Michael glanced up at the moon, furrowed his brow and shook his head. "No," he whispered. "I hoped you'd teach me how to fly."

"Fly? You mean so you can soar with the birds?"

"Yes! Would you?"

"I suppose I might."

"It would serve John right if you did."

"Why him?" I said, glancing at John in his bed.

"Because he doesn't believe that children *can* fly."

"Does he not?"

Michael frowned and glanced at his sleeping brother. "He laughed at me when I told him we'd been visited by a flying boy."

"So, you were only pretending to slumber when last I visited?"

Michael nodded.

I ruffled his hair. "You pretend well!"

"I practise every Christmas eve. Are you a pixie? Only when I told Wendy about you, she said you must be one."

"Oh? And what gave her that idea?" I said, glancing at her sleeping form.

"I told her how you wear clothes that are made from green leaves and moss." Michael stepped closer to me, and examined the moss that is stitched over my heart.

I made a hook with my hand, and it threw a shadow up on the wall. Michael glanced at this shadow and drew a deep breath.

I leaned closer to him and whispered, "The moss hides the tears that Captain Hook made when he slashed at me."

"Hook sounds like a rogue!" gasped Michael, then slapped a palm to his mouth.

I glanced at the beds. "It's alright. I don't believe you've woken them."

Michael lowered his voice again. "If not a pixie, then what are you?"

"Not what, but who." I bowed low and stood up straight. "I am Peter Pan, and I am at your service."

"Does that mean you have to teach me to fly? It would really serve John right if you did."

"For what?"

"For what he said about you."

"What did he say?"

Michael scratched his head. "That you're a *figment* of a child's over-active imagination."

"And what is a figment?"

Michael shrugged. "A *fig* that's *meant* to do something silly, perhaps?" Then he peered above my head all the way up to the ceiling.

I followed his gaze. "What is it you seek?"

"The strings… the ones that John says are always attached to children who *appear* to fly."

"Don't you believe?"

"Yes, of course. But now at least I can tell John that I had a good look… and couldn't see any."

I ruffled his hair again, and then floated up until my head almost touched the ceiling. "See? No strings," I whispered down at him.

"Michael? Who are you talking to?" said the voice of a sleepy girl.

"No one," whispered Michael. "Go back to sleep, Wendy."

I flew into the corner of the room where the light from the moon was weakest, and the shadows most pronounced. I watched Wendy sit up in bed and rub her eyes. "Have you been dreaming about pixies again?" she asked.

"I most certainly have not."

"Then go back to bed and stop talking to yourself. You know what John says about people who talk to themselves… that they'll go mad unless they stop it right away."

I tutted from the shadows. "And what does *John* know?" I whispered.

Wendy scrambled up onto her knees as though someone had pinched her. "Who… who said that?"

I floated down and landed on the carpet, bowed low, and then straightened up and assumed my most heroic pose. "I said it. Peter Pan."

Wendy's pretty mouth opened wide – so wide, in fact, that I put my fingers in my ears to block her coming scream.

"It's alright!" Michael whispered, preventing her. "This is Peter. And he's going to teach me to fly. Show her, Peter. Show Wendy how you can fly!"

I rose up and did several laps of the room like a fish darting around its bowl. I landed at the foot of her bed, and was surprised to see that far from closing, her mouth had opened wider still. She realised I was staring at the gaping hole in her face, and snapped it shut. I leaned forwards and whispered, "Answer me this: are you, perchance, any relation of the crocodiles?"

"A relation of the *whats*?" she replied loudly. Michael and I glanced at John, who shuffled a little under his blanket but did not wake.

I leaned closer still to Wendy and asked her again, "Are you a relation of the crocodiles? Only he snaps his mouth closed *just* as you do."

Wendy's mouth fell open again, and Michael shook her by her shoulders until it closed. "Peter's going to teach me to fly, and if you ask him nicely, maybe he'll teach you too."

Wendy looked at me, but her eyes failed to focus. "To answer your question," she murmured, "I don't believe that I am a relation of the crocodiles."

"It was a compliment," I said, "for the crocodile is a force for good in the Neverland. It hates pirates, you see. And it hates no pirate more than it hates James Hook. And if not for the ticking of the clock that the crocodile swallowed, it would have crept up on the captain and eaten the rest of him long ago. Do you follow?" The expressions on both their faces led me to believe they had difficulty following even the simplest things. "Well, then," I continued. "You'll just have to come to the Neverland and see for yourselves."

Wendy climbed off her bed and stood before me. I raised myself up on tiptoes and made myself slightly taller. She observed my face, then took a step back and studied my clothes.

"Don't call him a pixie. I don't think he likes it," said Michael.

"I didn't think he was a pixie," she said, looking closely at my ears. "How *old* are you?" she whispered.

I shrugged the shrug of the unfathomable. "None could say for sure, and some say I am as old as time itself."

Wendy's brow furrowed and she scratched her head. "But you're just a boy. No more than fourteen. My age."

I straightened my back and raised my chin. "Then I must have been fourteen when I decided *not* to grow any older."

"I'm afraid that deciding such things isn't possible," said Wendy.

"Neither is flying without wings, but you just saw Peter doing it," Michael pointed out.

"True," she said, stepping towards me and poking my chest.

"Stop that, Wendy! It's rude to poke people," whispered Michael.

"I have to check…" she poked.

"Check what?" asked Michael.

"That he's real…"

"Of *course* he is. What makes you think he isn't?"

"Only *everything* he says and *everything* he does."

"How would you like it if he poked at *your* chest?" I asked.

"I wouldn't. I'm a girl, so it would be inappropriate," she said, withdrawing her finger.

"Will you teach us both to fly before John wakes up?" asked Michael.

I shook my head and glanced at the window. "I must be getting back. It will soon be sun-up, and the cock's crow must be answered."

"Back where?" asked Wendy.

"The Neverland, and I must return without delay."

"What for?" asked Michael excitedly.

I drew my sword and spun about, expecting to see that a pirate had followed me somehow.

"What are you *doing*?" asked Wendy. "You'll have somebody's eye out with that thing."

I slid my sword back into my belt. "In the Neverland,

whenever anybody says *what for*, it means someone approaches who must be given what-for."

"Although that's great, it isn't what I meant," said Michael. "Why must you hurry back to the Neverland?"

"To find the Lost Boys."

Wendy smiled at me. "Do you always find them, Peter?"

I nodded. "Their day cannot start until I do." I floated up off the carpet. "I'll return soon enough. And that's when we'll see if it's still possible."

"See if what's still possible?" asked Michael.

"I know I can teach you to fly. You are young and your imagination has yet to permit boundaries." I looked at Wendy. "I believe there is still hope for you, too. As for your brother John, we shall just have to wait and see." I floated backwards towards the open window.

"And what should we tell John? About you, I mean?" asked Wendy.

"Tell him that if he doesn't believe children can fly, it may be too late for him to learn."

"That's not what I meant. What should we tell him about *you*?"

"Tell him everything!"

"But what if he doesn't believe us?" said Michael.

"Then tell him to prepare for my return, when he'll have little choice but to believe!"

Journal entry no. 4

The Neverland is the brightest star in the galaxy. Despite this truth, only those who remember how to *see* may look upon it. Adults leave the ability to *see* in childhood, and that's why they fail to see it, even through their most powerful telescopes. Just as well, for if they could see the Neverland they might build rocket ships one day and visit us. A disaster! They would change *everything*, and before long the Neverland would become The Land Where No One Ever Stops Worrying About Everything.

The Neverland's address is: The Neverland, Third (not the second!) Star on the Left, and then Straight On Till Morning. For those who still know how to look, it's the brightest star in the constellation of Asia Minor, the one that changes colour depending on the mood of its inhabitants. When white, the population of Neverland is mostly at rest. When flickering blue, it means that our spirits are high, and there is fun to be had in every quarter. But beware, reader, for when it flickers *scarlet* it means that murder and blood-lust are afoot. It was this scarlet flicker that greeted me upon my return from the Darlings. I flew through the outer atmosphere and made for the blue, kidney-shaped lagoon where Hook keeps his galleon. It is also where the Lost Boys are waiting to be found. On this particular morn, I spotted Tink sitting on a cloud, arms folded and with an expression like thunder. I landed beside her on the cloud and folded my arms.

"Why do you wear the face of someone who's been licking bat droppings off a rancid toad?" I asked.

Tink stood up. "Do you mind? And what time do you call this?"

"I do mind, for it can only be the time that I arrived back from the real world. Did my eyes deceive me, or was that a glow of scarlet I saw? Is trouble brewing?"

"Is trouble brewing, he asks. Tell me, *Peter*, where are you going now?" she said, tapping her foot impatiently upon the cloud.

"You *know* where I'm going. Is your question a trick one?"

"To find the Lost Boys?"

"Given the hour, where else?"

"Well, good luck with that!"

"What is wrong?"

"Hook has already found them!"

"But he can't have. Only I can find them. That is the earliest their day can begin."

"Their day has begun in earnest without you, and it's turning into their worst ever."

"What were they doing when Hook found them?"

"What else would the Lost Boys be doing just after the first cock has crowed, Peter? They were waiting to be found!"

Let that be a lesson to all who read this: if you're waiting to be found, chances are you will be. So remain alert, in case the finder should be not friend but foe.

"What are you going to do, Peter?" asked Tink. "Hook is going to make them walk the plank. They're to be the crocodile's breakfast."

I hurried to the edge of the cloud, crouched down, and observed Hook's galleon far below. "What do you *think* I'm going to do? I'm going to save them."

"Any idea how?"

"Hush now, fairy, and let me think."

I will leave myself there to think for a moment, reader, and share with you some facts about Hook's galleon. It is called the *Jolly Roger*, and it provides sanctuary to the most bloodthirsty pirates ever to roam the high seas. The *Jolly Roger* has three masts, the centremost of which is tall enough to pierce the clouds. Upon this mast hangs a sail vast enough to cast a black shadow the length and breadth of a football pitch. As I looked down from the cloud, this sail flapped and billowed over the hundreds of pirates manning its decks. I flew down from the cloud and saw Tootles, Slightly and Nibs, huddled amid a pack of baying pirates. The boys were stripped to their waists, and their hands had been tied behind their backs. It made my blood boil, reader, to see the red marks upon their backs where the cat o' nine tails had lashed at them. I scanned the calm waters for any sign of the crocodile, and beheld the beast some way off, moving at speed towards the plank. Hook likes to keep the belly of the crocodile always full. It has been his way ever since I cut off his hand and threw it into the crocodile's jaws. Since then the creature has craved the rest of him, which only goes to prove that there can be no accounting for a crocodile's taste. Now you understand why Hook provides the crocodile with a hearty breakfast every morning: it is the hope that it will leave him alone for the rest of the day.

Back to the events of earlier today…

One amongst the crew of ruffians spotted the crocodile's approach and called out, "Fetch the captain! The croc's here!"

I flew down, landed high up on the rigging, and shouted above the high winds, "And so too is Peter Pan!"

The Lost Boys looked up at me with tears in their eyes. As I smiled down at them, their eyes filled with watery hope. Drawing my sword, I floated down and landed upon the deck. Hook burst from his cabin with his first mate Smee. While Hook is tall and thin with a foul, bristling moustache, Smee is short and round with spectacles that are rounder still.

"Bad form, Pan!" growled Hook in a voice that sounded like approaching thunder.

I stamped a foot upon the deck. "And feeding helpless boys to crocodiles is *good form,* I suppose?"

"Helpless?" cried Hook. "Don't make me laugh! These three assassins have killed almost as many of my men as have volunteered to be the crocodile's breakfast."

"I see. So your men volunteer to be the croc's breakfast, do they?"

Hook nodded. "Of course. They're good men. Always keen to please their captain. Is that not so, men?" Hook's men made a low murmur that did not answer his question one way or another.

"See, Hook? You delude yourself. They are volunteered to be the crocodile's breakfast by you. And so great is their fear of you that they would sooner end up in its belly than cross you."

"As I said, they are good men." Hook looked suddenly mindful of something: the crocodile, and he listened for the ticking of the clock in its belly. We were all reminded of the creature, and listened but could hear no ticking. The silence of that rogue's galleon was broken by Hook himself. "Your day will come soon enough, *Pan*. In the meantime, stop interfering in business that is not your own. Fly away, little birdie, lest I clip your wings!" With that, he drew his cutlass.

I cut a figure of eight from the air. "Oh, I think this is my business, *Hook*."

"Don't be absurd. Since when was croc business any business of yours?"

"Since you decided to feed it not pirates, cereal or oats this morning, but my friends Nibs, Slightly and Tootles."

"I *found* them, Pan. And possession is nine-tenths of the law, which means they belong to me now. Is that not so, Smee?"

"That's right, Captain," said Smee, pulling his wide belt up over his hanging belly.

"And thanks to my generosity of spirit towards the crocodile," continued Hook, "the croc is to have something different for its breakfast."

"Think again!" I cried, "for the Lost Boys belong to no one."

"I'll decide what belongs to me and what does not aboard my own ship!" Hook stepped forwards and slashed at the shrinking space between us. I flew up onto the plank and observed the approach of the crocodile. Its size is equivalent to *two* lifeboats lashed together, and a bigger or more ferocious-looking beast you will never see. It was close enough now that all could hear its ticking. As I looked, the sound drained the colour from Hook's face. More than this, it had drained the strength from his legs, for he staggered sideways and grasped the hair of one of his men for support. Hook pulled the man's hair, and both their faces contorted in agony. "Be quick, men!" cried Hook, "and force those boys to walk the plank!"

"I won't let you do it!" I cried.

"Not a lot you can do about it, *Pan*," he said, as a hundred pirates spilled onto the deck like a tide that pushed the Lost Boys towards the plank.

Below, the crocodile gnashed its teeth and swished its tail, while above the mammoth sail billowed in the winds that now sensed our peril. Perhaps I should explain: the winds have always been a friend to us boys, and now they whistled an idea to me through a hole in the rigging. The whistle cried, "Cut down the main sail and use it to your advantage, Pan!"

I leapt and flew up with sword in hand and set about cutting out a great circle from the sail, one big enough to engulf the band of pirates that bundled the Lost Boys towards the plank. The severed circle of sail broke free, and the winds came at it from all angles and held it in place. I grasped hold of its edge, and flew down towards the mass of pirates with the sail clasped to my neck – the biggest cloak ever to be conjured in the imagination of any boy! Its shadow engulfed the pirates first, and their frightened faces looked up to see a great dark blanket descend upon them.

"Tink!" I called. "I will need your light!"

"And you shall have it, Peter!" Tink appeared not as girl with elfin face and wings, but as a tiny light that hovered close to my face. Hook looked on from a higher deck and shouted down to his men not to panic, but as soon as the sail fell and engulfed them in darkness, they began slashing at one another's shadows, believing them to be The Foes That Come In Sudden Darkness.

I scurried between their anxious feet and, led by Tink's light at the end of my nose, I made my way to the Lost Boys. "Hold still while I cut you free!" I said, slicing through the ropes that bound them with my dagger.

"I'm free, Peter!" shouted Nibs above the shrieks of pirates as they mistook friend for foe. Moments later, I had freed the Lost Boys.

"Nibs, you grab hold of my belt. Tootles, you grab Nib's belt, and Slightly, you take hold of Tootles. Are you all arranged?" I called behind me.

"Yes!"

"Yes!"

"Yes!"

"Go then, Tink! Lead us through the darkness and out of here!" Tink led us expertly through legs that swerved and stumbled, and soon enough we all four emerged into a sunlight that blinded us momentarily.

"This way," said Tink, tinkling for all she was worth. We followed the sound of her bell, climbed over the side of the ship, and fell into a lifeboat.

Shielding my eyes from the sun, I drew my sword and cut the ropes that lashed the boat to the side of the ship. It plunged down into the water with a splash. "To the oars before someone spots us!" I commanded. We each took up an oar, and made our getaway to the sound of Hook's bellows for calm, and the cries of pirates.

When we reached the shore, we hid the boat in some reeds and ran up a steep embankment. From our raised position, we looked out over the lagoon to where the pirates now sought what had moments before been the crocodile's intended breakfast. But to no avail, for its breakfast stood beside me, and all three courses looked the worse for wear.

"Well!" I said, slapping Slightly on his back. "A close shave was had by all, but all is well that ends well."

Nibs pointed to the *Jolly Roger*'s plank. "Not for all," he said. I knew his logic to be sound when I spied three pirates on their knees, hands clasped before them as they begged Hook not to make them walk it. "Do you imagine he'll show them mercy, Peter?" asked Tootles.

I shook my head. "Those men's names might just as well have been Toast, Orange Juice and Porridge. For a similar fate awaits all three now."

Tootles gulped. "It was almost our fate."

"It won't happen again, for I shall never be late finding you again."

"If we *had* ended up as breakfast for the crocodile, those

Darling children would have had a lot to answer for," said Nibs.

"Don't blame the Darlings; it was my fault. She awoke and I lost track of time."

"Who awoke?" asked Tootles.

"Wendy Darling," I said.

We heard the sound of Tink's bell and she appeared to us in human form, albeit with pointy ears, transparent wings and fairy frown. She folded her arms and said, "She woke, did she? And what did Wendy *darling* do when she found you in her room?"

Slightly patted me on the back. "She must have been impressed to find Peter in her room," he said.

"Impressed?" said Tink, looking me up and down.

"Yes," said Slightly. "After all, I doubt she wakes to find a genuine hero in her room very often."

"Or a peeping *Tom*," said Tink.

"I was not peeping," I pointed out.

"Really?" said Tink. "Then answer me this: were your eyes closed while you were there?"

"Of course not."

"Then shame on you for peeping!"

"Pan is no peeper!" I said.

"If you weren't peeping at Wendy *darling* then you must have been staring at her," said Tink, making her eyes bulge. The Lost Boys looked away from Tink who can look fearsome when she wants to.

"So what did Wendy Darling do when she saw you, Peter?" asked Tootles.

"Oh yes, Peter, what *did* Wendy *darling* do when she saw you?" said Tink, her green eyes as big and as round as saucers.

I sat upon the ground, placed my chin in my hands, and cast my mind back. "I can't remember everything, but… I'm sure she poked me."

Tink went bright red in her face. "She did *what?*"

"Poked me."

"Where?" said Tootles.

"In my chest."

"Once?" asked Tink.

I shook my head. "Truth be told, Wendy Darling poked me so many times I lost count."

"I hope you poked her back," said Nibs.

"No. She said it would be wrong to poke a girl in the chest."

"That's called double standards!" said Tink. "You know you can poke me anytime, don't you, Peter?" said Tink, smiling sweetly. The Lost Boys began to chuckle, but a glance from Tink silenced them.

"What did Wendy do after she'd finished poking you?" asked Nibs.

"Well, as I recall, her little brother Michael told her of my promise to teach him to fly. And he said that I might teach her to fly, too."

"And did she like the idea?" asked Slightly.

"I believe she did," I said.

"I *bet* she did," said Tink. "Well, I think if you do teach her to fly it would be perfectly mean of you."

"Silence, fairy! Teaching others to fly would be a noble act."

"Really? If that's so, then why haven't taught the Lost Boys to fly?"

"That's not fair," I protested. "You know I'm the only boy who's supposed to fly in the Neverland."

"And why is that?" asked Tink mischievously.

"You know as well as I that it is one of the unwritten rules of the land."

"But why?" asked Tink, a twinkle in her eye.

"Isn't it obvious? If everyone flies about the Neverland it would be transformed into an aviary for people."

"Peter has a point," said Slightly, gazing skyward.

Tink huffed. "The same could be said of teaching the children of the real world to fly. Yet you seem intent on teaching those little *darlings*."

"I have no choice. How else are they to come here?"
Tink fluttered her wings urgently and took to the air. "You
can't actually be considering bringing children from the real
world here?"

"Considering? No. Decided? Yes."

"You mustn't!" said Tink. "Not bringing children of the real
world here is another unwritten rule of the land. And you
can't cherry-pick which rules to obey and which to ignore."

"If it is an unwritten rule, then I think it a stupid one," I said.

"Why?" asked Tootles.

"Did we not all come from the real world once upon a time?
And did we not leave it because it did not agree with us?"

"But you all found your ways here *naturally*," said Tink.
"Which is nothing at all like bringing people here who have
no *right* to be here."

I folded my arms. "It doesn't seem fair to keep the Neverland
all to ourselves. Not all the time, Tink."

Tink threw her arms wide. "You know as well as I that the
Neverland is filled with children. They come here to stay
young forever, and to play in worlds created by *their*
imaginations – just as this world has been created by yours,
Peter. We've all seen their shadows or spotted their
reflections in water."

"I hear their laughter sometimes," said Tootles.

I patted him on the back. "We all do."

A voice above us asked, "Why are there so many

Neverlands?" We looked up at Tiger Lily. She was sitting astride a branch, bow in hand.

Tink fluttered her wings and flew up to her. "Because not all children want to live in a Neverland filled with dangerous Indians and pirates, a monster croc, and a hero called Peter Pan. They choose to inhabit the Neverlands of their own imaginations."

"Do you think that children from these other Neverlands see us sometimes?" asked Tootles.

"I know they do," said Tink. I rose to my feet, walked to the edge of the precipice, and gazed out over the lagoon.

"What is it, Peter?" asked Nibs.

"I've felt as though something has been missing from our Neverland of late."

"Missing?" said Tink.

I turned to face them. "Yes, child visitors from the real world... but not for long," I said, flying up over their heads.

"But what good will it do us bringing them here?" said Tink.

"I think it will do *them* good. For when they are to return to the real world and grow up, they might always remember us, and maybe that will help to keep their imaginations alive."

That night when I returned to the Darlings's house, I thought I'd find them excited about learning to fly. I landed on the carpet in the middle of the room, placed my hands on my hips, and looked from one to the other. Far from pleased to see me, Wendy and Michael looked as miserable as pigs deprived of dirt. And worse still, their brother John sat on his bed clutching a cricket bat, an expression of grim intent on his face.

"It's alright, Peter," said Wendy. "John isn't going to hit you with his bat."

"I might," said John nervously.

"See! I told you Peter was real, John," said Michael, pointing at me.

John got up, and although a year younger than Wendy, he stood just as tall. He was a serious-looking boy with reddish hair that lay upon a large forehead. He raised his bat with shaky hands and asked impertinently, "Are you friend or foe?"

I was taken aback and so took a step back. "Tell me this," I asked, spreading my arms wide, "would a *foe* fly astronomical distances across space and time to teach the gift of flight?"

As I said, John's forehead is large, and I deduced that his brain must be large also. I reconsidered this when he said, "Liar! Flying astronomical distances across space and time isn't possible."

I cocked my head at him and observed him as though he may be broken. "Why would you say such things to someone who does so regularly?"

"For starters," he said, clutching his bat, "you can't fly through space because nobody can."

"And why not?"

"Because there's no oxygen in space, so you couldn't breathe," he said uncertainly, looking to his siblings for agreement.

"Oxygen?" I said.

"Air! Air to breathe!" John's exasperation at trying to comprehend these things seemed to drain him of the very oxygen he needed, and so he sat on his bed, gasping for more.

"I stand before you as proof that these things *are* possible. And that is surely good news," I pointed out helpfully.

John shook his head. "How can finding out that everything I ever read in my science books isn't true be a *good* thing?"

"It's exciting, surely!" said Wendy.

John began to thump the side of his head with a flat palm. "*Good*? If it's really true, it means I must rearrange everything."

"Oh, stop beating yourself up," Wendy suggested.

"Sterling advice, Wendy!" I said. "And count your lucky stars, because it could be so much worse."

"My poor troubled brother won't stop thumping his own head. How could it be worse?"

"Well, he might be thumping his head with his bat. I remember how one of Hook's crew beat himself up with a bat once…" I paused and saw that I had their attention; even John had paused his thumping to listen. "I think it best if I say no more about it. He hit his own head with his bat until he could hit it no more and, well, let's just say the resulting sight was not a pretty one."

"But why would he beat himself up with a *bat?*" asked John.

I shrugged. "Hook told him to do it."

"By why?" asked Wendy.

"As entertainment, why else?"

"Hook? Who's Hook?" asked John.

"The captain of the pirates," said Michael, pleased to know something his brother didn't for once.

"Wendy?" I said, narrowing my eyes. "Why have you and Michael grown so heavy of heart?"

Wendy went to the window and gazed up at the stars. "What does it matter to you?" she whispered.

I stood beside her. "It is important that you reverse your melancholy, and without delay."

"Why is it, Peter?"

"Isn't it obvious? Learning to fly with a heavy heart is like setting sail with your ship's anchor dropped, or trying to ride a sledge back up a snow-covered hill. You do still want to learn, don't you?"

Wendy gazed at me with watery eyes. Michael came and stood beside her. He took hold of her hand and I watched a tear roll down his cheek. "What has happened to make you all so miserable?" I asked.

"Are you sure you want to know, Peter?" said Wendy. "After all, you're so carefree... I'd hate to ruin that by making your heart heavy."

"I do not think that you can."

"It's Kenneth," said Michael, squeezing his sister's hand.

"Kenneth?" I asked, looking from one to the other.

"He's the boy who lives next door," said Wendy. "He's been unwell, and about a week ago, just after your last visit, he lost his fight and left us."

My hand went to the hilt of my sword. "Was it pirates? Did they follow me?"

"Oh, Peter. Don't you know there are no pirates here? Kenneth hadn't been well for some time."

Michael wiped a tear from his cheek. "He'd been staying at Great Ormond Street," he said.

"Great Ormond Street?" I asked.

"It's a hospital," said Wendy. "One where they look after poorly children. We were looking forward to visiting him, but on the morning of our visit, Mother told us we must prepare for the worst."

From behind us John said, "They said we'd get a chance to say goodbye. And we all promised Kenneth that we would. We took oaths. So you see, we've let him down."

"How old was Kenneth?" I asked.

"He was to be thirteen next month," said Wendy.

"And did he possess a good imagination? Be sure and speak with an honest heart," I said, pointing at Wendy's.

Wendy smiled. "Oh, yes. He had the best imagination! He used to play with his collection of toy knights for hours."

John became animated. "Do you remember how he would imagine he was a knight in Camelot, Wendy?" He put down his bat and slid open the drawer of his bedside table. "He gave me his favourite toy knight," he said sorrowfully, taking out the wooden figure of a knight no larger than his thumb.

"It's a fine knight," I said.

"Yes. Kenneth swapped it for one of my toy soldiers. We made a pledge, you see…"

"A pledge?"

"To look after each other's toy, and to swap them back only once Kenneth was well again. Only that's never going to happen now." John wiped the back of his hand over his eyes.

"And what's more," he continued, "the hospital has lost Kenneth's favourite possessions, *including* the soldier I swapped with him."

I stepped towards John and looked down at the wooden knight in his grasp. "Listen well, all of you," I said. "Kenneth's possessions were not lost. He has taken them with him … cock-a-doodle-doo!" I whispered.

"Peter!" said Wendy crossly. "How could you be so insensitive when our friend has died?"

My smile broadened. "Were you not listening? Your friend is not dead. He has gone to a better place."

"Yes, we know. To heaven," said Michael with a sigh.

"There is no need to be glum. I'd wager one of the Lost Boys that Kenneth is in Camelot right now, and that he has become the brave knight he always wanted to be."

"Are you saying he's in the Neverland?" asked Michael.

I nodded.

"If that's true, then might you see him there?" asked Michael.

"I might, but only as a fleeting shadow. Or I might hear his laughter."

"Kenneth laughed a lot," said Wendy.

"Then I expect it's only a matter of time before I do."

"And if we go with you to the Neverland, might we hear him laugh?" asked Michael.

"If you listen for it, I don't see why not."

"I don't believe you," said John sadly.

"But you *must* believe me."

John lay on his bed and faced the wall. "Why? What difference will it make?"

"Don't you want to fulfil your pledge to say goodbye?" I asked.

John looked at me over his shoulder. "Of course. Wendy and Michael never told me how cruel you are."

"Cruel? How can helping you fulfil such an important pledge be cruel?"

John sat up and glared at me. "But you can't! Kenneth is gone and we'll never see him again. Stop saying these things."

"But we might," said Michael eagerly, "if we go to the Neverland."

"There is no Neverland. Not really. Don't be such a gullible child!" said John.

"John," implored Wendy. "Keep your voice down, otherwise you'll wake Mother and Father."

"Maybe I should wake them. At least they'd put a stop to this."

"Would you like me to bring *proof* that the Neverland exists?" I asked.

"Good luck with that," said John quietly.

I took off and flew three times around the room at such speed that I appeared as a blur. As I flew I plucked Kenneth's knight from John's hand without him knowing. The blur became Pan by the window. "How about I go one better? And return with proof that Kenneth lives on in the Neverland!"

"You're insane!" said John, sitting up.

"Maybe so, yet prove it I shall! Otherwise your heavy hearts will keep you grounded in the real world forever." I flew from the window, soared above London, and crowed so loudly that inhabitants for miles around might hear me. Then I fixed my gaze on the star I knew to be home, and sped towards it with Kenneth's knight in my grasp.

Journal entry no. 7

I arrived back just before sun-up, swooped down into the forest, and shot up the side of the tallest tree in Neverland: Tink's tree. She lives in a fairy castle way up in its highest branches. Although no bigger than a box in which a girl might crouch, when Tink transforms into a speck of light she has three hundred rooms to choose from.

If she is woken suddenly from her slumber, Tink is transformed into her human-fairy form. At such times, her palace becomes a single room, only large enough for her to sit with head bowed and legs drawn to her chest. I had just woken her by tapping on her castle's roof, and so this is how I found her. "Oh, it's you, Peter," she said, a green eye filling a window in the attic. "You woke me from a delightful dream, so this had better be important."

"It's of the utmost importance," I said, holding the toy knight up to the window.

Her eye narrowed. "All I see is stupid little knight."

"Look again, for this is no ordinary knight."

Tink yawned. "If you must wake me long before the first cock has crowed, I'd appreciate your telling me why before it has a chance to."

"As you wish. This toy knight belongs to *Kenneth,*" I said, as though confiding a secret.

"I've never heard of him."

"Maybe not, but I'll wager you've heard his laughter. I am told he laughs often and loud."

Tink's eye focused on the toy knight in my hand. "Are you saying it belongs to one of the nether children?"

"That is precisely what I'm saying, and it will therefore have his aura all over it."

"That's nice."

"Nice? Don't you see? This is the first time we've had something that belongs to one of the nether children. And we might use it to find a way to into his Neverland."

"Why? Is there something wrong with our own Neverland?"

I shook my head. "We must return this toy to Kenneth."

"Why must we?"

"Because *he* is its rightful owner."

"I see. So you want to do that which has *never* been done, just to return a silly toy? Is that all?"

"No, it isn't. We must swap this toy knight for a toy soldier that belongs to John."

"John?"

"John Darling."

Tink's eye narrowed. "Wendy *darling's* brother?"

"Exactly. His heart has grown heavy, but will be lightened when I find his soldier and return it to him. It will help to prove that his friend lives on in the Neverland."

Tink's eye closed.

"Tink! Wake up! This is the perfect opportunity for us to help all the Darlings shed the burden of their heavy hearts."

Tink's eye opened slowly. "Ah well, just so long as all the little *darlings* are happy. Now, if you don't mind, I'm going to catch up on my forty winks." Tink's eye vanished from the window and I heard a faint tinkling from within as she returned to her bedchamber.

I stood and banged on the castle's roof. "Oh no, you don't! You're to come out and help me. You should have seen the gloom that losing their friend has caused the poor Darlings."

Tink's castle began shuddering, and her voice came from within. "If you want to help the *poor darlings,* then nobody's stopping you!"

I sat cross-legged on a branch and placed my head in my palms. "Tink," I said, "of all the fairies I have met, I believe you to be the wisest."

"Go on," said Tink, her voice softer now.

"And because you're the wisest, I shall need your help in finding the solution to finding Kenneth's Neverland."

There was a flash of light and Tink appeared, straddling the top of her fairy castle. "Do you mean it? Am I wisest fairy you know?"

"How could you ever doubt it?"

"Anything else?" said Tink, fluttering her eyelids and creating fairy dust that made me sneeze.

"Else?" I said.

"Look at me…" said Tink, leaning back on her palms and extending her long neck. "Am I not a beautiful fairy?"

"The most beautiful."

"And do you think me more beautiful than Wendy Darling?"

"Do you really need you ask? How can a human compete with a fairy when the competition is beauty?"

"It is Tiger Lily's help you need," she confided with a smile

"Tiger Lily's? She is best known for her skills with bow and arrow, not wisdom."

"It's her grandfather, Chief Hiawatha, that you must speak with. His soul is the oldest and wisest in the Neverland. If anybody knows of a way to move between Neverlands, it will be him."

"I knew I must come and speak to you first, and that you wouldn't let me down. Thank you, Tink." Tink's face was lit by a smile. Emboldened by it, I added, "We must go and speak with Tiger Lily now."

"Now?" said Tink, her smile vanishing.

"Yes. Were you not listening? There is no time to lose."

"But Peter, you know as well as anyone how dangerous it is

to go to Indian Creek before sun-up. Have you forgotten the last time? They mistook you for a pirate and shot you with an arrow."

I rubbed at my backside. "How could I forget? I am reminded of our misadventure every time I sit on a damp log."

"So we wait for sun-up?

"No. There'll be no sneaking around this time. We'll fly straight to Tiger Lily's tee-pee."

"We?"

"Of course. This adventure is much too important not to have you by my side." Tink's smile returned in spades.

There are hundreds of teepees at Indian Creek. Tiger Lily is the Chief's granddaughter, and she is a princess, so her teepee forms part of the centremost ring. The trees on the approach to Indian Creek are always full of snipers on the lookout for pirates. We waited for a cloud to float across the front of both moons, and then swooped down in the darkness and landed outside Tiger Lily's teepee.

Once inside, we found Tiger Lily asleep beside her sister Dainty Rose Petal. Whenever Tiger Lily complains that her name doesn't make her sound like a true warrior, I remind her of her sister's name. I tiptoed up to Tiger Lily, lying asleep upon the ground, and did my best not to wake Dainty Rose Petal, but I should have remembered how Tiger Lily says her sister likes to sleep with one eye open. The next thing I knew, Dainty Rose Petal was upon me with an axe, intent on cleaving my head in two. In a flash, I drew my sword and steel clanked against steel. The sound woke Tiger

Lily, who cried, "Dainty Rose Petal! Stop it! Don't you recognise him? He's my friend, Peter!" Dainty Rose Petal snarled at me and backed away. Nibs says she's so aggressive because she feels she has to compensate for her name. Once, the Lost Boys and I drew straws to decide who would put that question to her. I made sure that I drew the short straw, as Dainty Rose Petal would have killed any of the others for asking it.

"Why are you here, Peter?" asked Tiger Lily.

"I have come seeking your help."

Tiger Lily blushed. "You have?"

Tink flew from my pocket and transformed into her human-fairy self. "It was my help he sought first," she said, her nose raised high. Her nose lowered quickly enough when she noticed Dainty Rose Petal glaring at her. "That one has anger management issues," said Tink, producing her wand.

"Never mind her. What is it you need my help with, Peter?"

"I need to ask your grandfather the Chief something, and it has to be before the sun rises. It is a matter of great urgency." I explained the need to find Kenneth and swap his knight for John's toy soldier, and how John's soldier must be returned to him. "In this way the Darlings will know their friend lives on. Their heavy hearts will be lifted and they can learn to fly."

"Those poor Darling children," said Tiger Lily. "Their hearts sound so heavy with sorrow. Don't you think so, Dainty Rose Petal?" Tiger Lily's sister hurled her axe into the wooden tent pole as though she knew better than anyone how to put the Darlings out of their misery.

Only Tink was amused by this. "You know," said Tink, "I think your sister is onto something. If I were her I would hurl the axe at Wendy *darling* first. There's no need to look at me like *that*, Peter. Sometimes you have to be cruel to be kind."

Tiger Lily shook her head and stood up. "I'll go and wake my grandfather now."

Several minutes later, Tiger Lily poked her head inside the teepee. "Chief Hiawatha will see you now," she said.

Chief Hiawatha's tent was spacious and round, and smelt of tobacco and herbs. The Chief sat at its middle, puffing on a pipe, and looking just as old and wise as you would expect an Indian chief to. Tiger Lily, Tink and I sat down, forming a circle with him.

"Tell me, how may I help you?" he said, puffing away. I placed Kenneth's toy knight between my thumb and forefinger, and held it up so that Chief Hiawatha could see it clearly. "It is a fine toy knight," he said.

"Indeed. It has come from the real world, and I seek its owner who now resides in the Neverland."

"Finding him should not prevent any difficulty for Peter Pan," asserted the Chief.

"Normally, I would agree. But the boy I seek is not in our Neverland; he is in another."

The Chief smiled and nodded sagely. "Are your reasons for travelling to another's Neverland noble?" he asked.

"Yes, for there are children in the real world whose heavy hearts I wish to lighten. I believe that I can achieve this by taking them proof that their friend has gone to a better place. I must therefore swap this knight for a soldier that their friend has taken with him."

"Your cause is indeed a noble one," puffed the Chief.

"They really are *such* little darlings," said Tink through clenched teeth.

"This fairy has anger management issues," observed the Chief.

"Forgive her. She is a work in progress," I said.

"Oh, that's rich," said Tink. "I'm as sweet as a sleeping babe on a summer's morn compared to Dainty Rose Petal."

"It's true," said Chief Hiawatha. "Dainty Rose Petal is a work in progress too."

"And not a lot of progress has been made," murmured Tink.

"Hush now, fairy, please! This is important. Let Chief Hiawatha speak." I looked at the Chief, whose eyes were now tightly closed. "Tiger Lily? Is he sleeping?" I asked.

Tiger Lily shook her head. "He's thinking."

"About the problem at hand?" I said hopefully.

Tiger Lily nodded, then crossed her fingers.

Some minutes later, and with his eyes still closed, Chief Hiawatha said, "I have been away consulting with the spirits of my forefathers."

"And are they well?" I asked politely.

"The spirits of my ancestors are in rude health. Thank you for asking."

I leaned closer to the Chief. "Think nothing of it. And?"

"And they tell me there is but one way to move between our own Neverland and the others at this time." The Chief opened his eyes and looked at me. "But the way is dangerous."

I puffed out my chest, but given the late hour, I resisted the urge to crow. "It's a good thing that *dangerous* ought to be my middle name, then," I said.

"If it were, then people would mistake you for a faulty cooking utensil," mumbled Tink. Although true, the Chief and I ignored her comment.

"My ancestors have informed me that you must find the clock with four faces."

"And where is this clock?"

"Peter Pan should not need to ask such a question," he replied.

I slapped my forehead. "Of course! Hook's cabin!" The peculiar truth is this, reader: Hook has stolen all the clocks in the Neverland so as not to be frightened unnecessarily by a ticking that does not come from the crocodile's stomach. In this way, he can go about his daily business of theft and murder without a care.

Tiger Lily shifted nervously where she sat. "If Hook has such a powerful clock, why hasn't he used it to plunder other Neverlands, Grandfather?" she asked.

Chief Hiawatha shrugged. "It can only be that he is uncertain of how to harness its power."

I felt my heart begin to race. "Then it must be removed from Hook's cabin without delay. And once we have it, how might *I* harness its power?"

"It must be conveyed to the highest point in the Neverland," said the Chief. "Once there, the toy that belongs to the boy you seek must be placed inside it. If the object rightfully belongs to the boy, a portal will open within the clock's face."

"A portal that leads to his Neverland?"

Chief Hiawatha nodded.

We needed a plan to steal the clock with four faces from Hook's cabin. I do not know about you, but I find that plans are best come by whilst pacing and slashing at imaginary pirate foes. I felt the gaze of the Lost Boys upon me as I blocked and parried. Meanwhile, Tink danced the part of Juliet in the ballet of *Romeo and Juliet,* as this helps *her* think. Mercifully, she long ago gave up asking me to dance the part of her Romeo. During her dance, she spun across my path, and I was forced to freeze mid-swipe.

"I have an idea!" she said, spinning to a stop. I slid my sword back into my belt. "Well then, let's have it."

"Hook's first mate, Smee," she said quietly, taking off her ballet shoes. "We must kidnap him."

"Why *that* chubby pirate?" I asked.

"He's the only one who's allowed to go in and out of Hook's cabin unchallenged. My spies inform me that he even has his own set of keys."

"You think he can be convinced to join us?" said Nibs.

"Of course not," Tink admonished him. "That round pirate is bad through and through. But if we kidnap him, I can turn

Peter into his doppelgänger. Then, using Smee's keys, he can enter Hook's cabin and find the clock he seeks. Well?" she asked me, "what do you think of my plan?"

I placed my fisted hands on my hips and cock-a-doodle-dooed.

We soon discovered that opportunities to kidnap Smee were few and far between. Tiger Lily was tasked with spying on him, and she reported that the only time he was alone was when he visited the ship's latrine. "He insists on being alone when he uses it," she said. "So he can read *The Pirate Times* in peace."

I should explain that when pirates go to the toilet, they hang their bottoms over the stern of their ship. On pirate ships this is known as the poop rail, and it explains why you never find mermaids swimming below that location – at least none with any self-esteem. "If we're going to abduct Smee from the poop rail, we shall need a boat," I said.

"We still have the one we used to escape Hook's ship the other day," said Nibs.

"Good. We will row out to the ship's stern, where I will fly up and knock Smee unconscious. I will need a rope to carry him down to the waiting boat."

"We have plenty of rope, Peter," said Tootles.

I placed my hand on my chin in a thoughtful way. "I will also need to borrow your umbrella, Tootles."

"Why? Are you expecting rain?" he asked.

"Not rain, but something far worse."

The penny dropped (in much the same way as the poop might) and everyone grimaced.

As soon as night fell, the Lost Boys and I set out in the lifeboat for Hook's galleon. It was a windless night and, with the exception of the splish of our oars, the water in the lagoon was flat. As we drew nearer the ship's stern, the splish of our oars was accompanied by the occasional splash of... well, I'm sure you can work out what, reader.

Once we'd reached the stern, I tied the rope about my waist, opened the umbrella, and flew up close to the ship so as not to be spotted by look-outs. Tink's spies had confirmed that Smee likes to sit on the poop rail at 11.15pm. From the position of the two moons, I judged the time to be 11.14pm when I arrived below the poop rail. I summoned my courage and peered around the umbrella's edge. A dark shadow moved over the rail above me. If Tootles's umbrella was to be spared, I had absolutely had no time to lose. I dropped it, flew up, and knocked Smee unconscious with a blow from the hilt of my sword. I tied the rope to the poop rail, threw Smee over my shoulder, and climbed back down the rope to the waiting boat. "Bind his hands and feet, boys! And be quick about it!" I whispered.

Journal entry no. 9

Smee was still unconscious when we got back to the lagoon. Tink knelt down beside him, examining him from the 'tip' of his flattened nose to the heels of his brown boots. "You aren't going to be a handsome boy for a time, Peter," she said.

"He isn't even going to be a boy," said Tootles.

"I will be. It's just an illusion."

Tink stood up and held her wand towards me. "Ready?" she asked.

I raised my chin. "Smee me," I said gamely, doing my best to look comfortable with my suggestion. Once Tink had cast her spell, I beheld the open-mouthed gazes on the faces of all present. I ran a hand down my nose. It was no longer short and slightly upturned, but large and flat and seemingly intent on taking over my entire face.

Tink stepped forward to examine her handiwork. "If the inhabitants of the Neverland had mothers, you could fool Smee's," she said. "But try not to speak, as you still sound like yourself."

"Alright."

Tink looked a little woozy, as though she'd been drinking

fairy brandy. "You had best get going, Peter," she yawned. "Keeping you like this is a drain on my energy. When I fall asleep, which I must eventually, the spell will be broken and you will be revealed as your true self." A moment later, an apparently fat, short-sighted pirate was flying at speed towards Hook's galleon.

I swooped low and skirted the still dark water. A look-out was up in the crow's nest. If you've never seen a crow's nest, it's a wicker basket large enough to hold a skinny pirate. The skinny pirate was facing east, so I approached from the west and landed silently upon the deck. I climbed some steps that led up to Hook's cabin, and took the key from my pocket. The old key turned in the lock with a *clink*. As the door creaked open into Hook's cabin, my ears were assaulted by the sound of a thousand ticking clocks. The entrance to his cabin was dark, but towards the rear some candles lit up a platform upon which Hook's slumbering form could be seen. He was on his back, his arm dangling from the bed and his razor-sharp hook resting upon the ground. Behind and encircling him were a dozen shelves that went from floor to very high ceiling. As I crept closer, I could see the bristles of Hook's moustache moving as he breathed in and out. I climbed the final step and looked down at him, thinking it the perfect opportunity to rid our Neverland of its greatest villain. I felt for my sword... but it wasn't there! I found only Smee's pistol. I reconsidered Hook's immediate fate and whispered, "Killing one's greatest foe while he slumbers would be bad form, and it would make me no better than he." I crept past the bed to the shelves of clocks beyond, scanning them for a clock with four faces. I saw it, six shelves above me: a clock with four sides, a face on each, like a miniature of Big Ben in London. I was about to float up to retrieve it when a sleepy voice said, "Smee?" I turned to see Hook sitting up on his side, head in palm and black curls about his face and shoulders. "I'm glad you're here, Smee," he said sleepily.

I lowered my voice as best I could. "Evenin', Cap'n,' I said.

Hook yawned. "Is that a frog in your throat, Smee?"

"Aye, Cap'n," I said. "The little blighter's been there all evenin'."

Hook retrieved a pistol from under his pillow. "Come closer, Smee," he said, cocking the pistol, "and let me blast the blighter where it lurks."

I shook my head and lowered my voice as best I could under the circumstances. "There's no need to waste a shot from your pistol, Cap'n."

Hook waved his pistol about his head. "If you're sure. Tell me, Smee, what are you doing in my cabin at this hour?"

"I couldn't sleep, Cap'n. And when I can't sleep, I like to, ah… wind your clocks."

"I never knew that about you, Smee. But then again, I've never awoken and caught you in the act before."

"Right you are, Cap'n. Now go back to sleep. Big day tomorrow."

"Big day tomorrow, you say, Smee?"

"Biggest of days."

Hook lay back down. "I'll take you at your word. Smee?"

"Yes, Cap'n?"

"Since you're here, would you mind combing your old Captain's hair like you used to?"

"*What?*" I croaked.

"I know I told you never to speak of it, but once more couldn't hurt. You remember how quickly I used to nod off? I still have the brush; it's in the bottom drawer of my chest."

Reader, I would prefer to skip the scene where, as part of this important covert mission, I was left with little choice but to brush Hook's hair until he fell asleep. And so I will jump to the part where the dread pirate in question was snoring soundly...

By the time Hook was snoring, my chubby fingers had grown longer and thinner, and I knew that Tink's spell must be wearing off. I tossed aside the comb, flew up to the sixth shelf, and grabbed the clock with four faces.

Outside I flew straight and true for the highest peak in the Neverland. By the time I arrived, I was myself again. I placed the knee-high clock upon the ground, and admired the views of the Neverland around me. To the east, the sun's first rays cast their light upon deep valleys, while to the south they reflected off seas of blue, and to the north they lit forests of green where animals of both fact and fiction have always roamed. I shall leave what I beheld in the west to your own imagination. I reached into my pocket and took out Kenneth's toy knight. "And now I must bid you farewell, my Neverland, and embark on a journey to another. But fear not, for I shall return soon enough with the evidence I need to prove that Kenneth lives on."

"You do know that talking aloud to yourself is a sign of insanity, don't you?" said Tink from behind me.

I looked over my shoulder at her. "I didn't see you there."

"Obviously not."

"What are you doing here, Tink? Aren't you exhausted? I thought you'd be sleeping."

"I've been sleeping, and now I've come to instruct you in the ways of the clock." Tink knelt and opened two of its faces: the one that faced east and the one that faced west, thereby creating a passage between the two. I knelt beside her and peered through to the other side – to a world where the light of an afternoon was far brighter than that of the sleepy morning in my own Neverland.

"You have the toy knight that belongs to the nether boy?" Tink asked.

I nodded.

"Then place it inside, as Chief Hiawatha told you."

I did as she instructed, then stuck my hand all the way through the clock and wriggled my fingers about. "My hand is in Kenneth's Neverland?" I asked.

"If that toy belongs to him."

"It does."

"If what you say is true, then once you've passed through to the other side, the toy will guide you to its owner."

"The entrance is much smaller than I imagined it to be. You know of a way to make it larger?"

Tink shook her head knowingly. "I must make you smaller."

"How much smaller?"

Tink replied by bringing her thumb and forefinger close together.

If truth be told, I didn't much like being bumblebee-sized, and I wondered how they manage to remain so upbeat while collecting pollen. Thankfully, I wasn't so small for long, and once through to the other side, felt myself extending like a telescope. Within seconds I was my old self again, and soaring over Kenneth's Neverland in the sunlight of a bright afternoon.

This Neverland was very different from my own, its landscape more in tune with the English countryside than the tropical isle of my own Neverland. As far as the eye could see, it looked deserted of people. I took Kenneth's toy knight from my pocket, flew up to just below the clouds, and held it above my head. "Light the way to your earthly owner!" I commanded. A light shone from the knight that disappeared over the horizon. I flew at the speed of sound in that direction, and cock-a-doodle-dooed as my sonic booms echoed across the green meadows below.

I saw something that caused me to slow from hundreds of miles per hour to a standstill in a second: it was a fire-breathing dragon as tall as Tink's oak tree! Galloping towards this fearsome beast was a knight dressed in silver armour and riding a black stallion. The dragon opened its wings and breathed fire down upon the knight, whose horse reared up and threw him to the ground. The knight rolled from the path of the fire, and the ground was left scorched and smoking. I flew into the dragon's line of sight and drew my sword. I had hoped to distract it, and it worked: it roared at me and its breath brought with it fire to roast me. I flew up out of its path, and then down upon the dragon where I slashed at its scaly chest. Meanwhile, the knight had climbed back on his horse and was holding a lance. He held it up to get my attention and beckoned to me. I flew in his direction, the dragon's fiery breath nipping at my heels. As the dragon spun about, the knight shot forwards upon his horse, caught the beast unawares, and buried his lance deep in its chest. The dragon roared and threw its head from side to side, then breathed its last and slumped to the ground. "Well fought, sir knight!" I called from high above.

The knight climbed down from his horse and took off his helmet, and I could see he was a boy no taller than I. "Well fought yourself, sir!" he said.

I floated down and landed beside him. "Only too glad to come to the aid of a fellow hero. I've little doubt that the beast had it coming?"

The knight strode to the body of the beast and kicked it. "You have no idea. This monster has been killing the good citizens of Camelot for many a year. And now, thanks to your timely distraction and my trusty lance, they can once again sleep easy in their beds." He kicked the dragon one more time, I supposed for luck, then turned to me. "And now, flying boy dressed in the leaves of the forest, what might I do for you in return?"

"A timely question. You could point me in the direction of Kenneth."

The knight looked puzzled, as though some unfathomable mystery had been laid before him. "*Kenneth*?" he murmured.

"Yes. I do not know his other names. I know only that his Christian name is Kenneth, and that he hails from a town called London in the real world."

"*Kenneth?*" murmured the knight again, as though his faculties had deserted him. His eyes opened wide as though a penny had dropped and raised a pair of shutters. "What a small land it must be, for *I* am *Sir* Kenneth."

"The land is indeed small," I said, smiling.

"Why do you look at me with such knowing eyes?" he asked. "Surely, I cannot be the Kenneth you seek? I have been *Sir* Kenneth for as long as I can remember."

I stepped forward and placed a hand on the confounded knight's shoulder. "And how far back *can* you remember?"

Sir Kenneth licked his dry lips. "Truth be told," he said, "now you mention it, I cannot remember as far back as I imagined I might."

"Come with me," I said, leading him to a tree that had been felled by the dragon's death throes.

We sat side by side on the tree, and with his gaze fixed firmly upon the ground he said, "You think *I* am the Kenneth you seek?"

"I grow more certain of it with every moment that passes."

"And who might you be?" he asked.

I told him that I was Peter Pan, and of that there could be no doubt. I took the toy knight from my pocket and placed it in his hand. He felt it for a moment, like a blind boy reading Braille, and then looked down at it. "I *know* this toy," he said.

"That's because it's yours… it's the knight you gave to your friend John. You remember him?"

"*John?*"

"That's right. Brother to Wendy and…"

"… *Michael?*"

I smiled. "Your earthly past is coming back to you! I can see it in your eyes."

Kenneth stood up suddenly, as though startled, and peered closely at the toy in his hand. "Tell me, Peter, do I have something of John's?"

"Yes!" I said, standing and clapping him on the back.

He looked around uncertainly. "And has he come to collect it?" he asked.

"No, he couldn't come. Leaving the earthly realm would have been impossible as he has grown too heavy of heart. But as you rightly say, you have something of his that, should I return it to him, will relieve him of his sorrow."

He looked at me, such a serious look, and said, "Is it a toy soldier?"

"Yes."

"Then we must find it so you can return it to him without delay."

Sir Kenneth was on his white charger and galloping at great speed towards Camelot. I flew above him, occasionally shooting on ahead and then doubling back to fly alongside him. Before long the walls of that fabled city appeared and spanned the horizon from east to west as far as the eye could see. He rose up in his saddle and coaxed his horse to greater speeds, then pulled on the reins and brought the horse to a thundering halt. He shielded his eyes from the sun and called up to me. "Peter!" he cried. "It would be best if you did not fly into Camelot, but rode on the back of my horse."

I swooped down towards him. "But why?"

"The good people of Camelot have never seen a flying boy of the forest. It may give them cause for alarm. They are kind but simple folk, and therefore they are frightened of the unknown rather than awed by it, as they should be."

"Agreed! I will trust your judgement," I said, landing behind him on his horse.

Upon our approach, the drawbridge was lowered and hundreds of townsfolk spilled out for news of the dragon. Sir Kenneth sat proud and straight in his saddle. "It has been slain!" he said. "The dragon can harm you no more!" The townspeople cheered him. "Enjoy this time of peace!" Sir

Kenneth went on, "but be ever mindful that a new threat may come one day to replace the dragon." The crowd fell silent. "But fear not!" cried Sir Kenneth, "for whatever foes are thrown against us, they will be vanquished just as the dragon has been! This, my friends, is my solemn pledge to you all!"

We rode through the streets of Camelot to raised hats and cheers, and arrived at the tower where Sir Kenneth lives. We climbed its many steps, and at its top entered his private chamber: a luxurious room with arrow slits cut into its thick stone walls. Between these slits were hung tapestries depicting great battles where Sir Kenneth could be seen in the thick of the action. All about the room were shelves with medieval weapons: axes, crossbows, maces and lances. Sir Kenneth went to a bowl and splashed water on his muddy face. I scanned the room for the toy soldier I'd come to find, but I could see no toys. The truth is this: Sir Kenneth's toys were *everywhere*. In the Neverland, toys are the real thing.

"It's a fine collection of weaponry, is it not, Peter?" he asked.

I picked up a long sword and swung it skilfully. "The best I have ever seen!"

He cast his gaze about his chamber. "I don't recall ever seeing John's soldier. If I had, I would have remembered him. What if it isn't here?"

"It is here. You brought it. I know you did."

Sir Kenneth's gaze found his bed – a four-poster with a canopy, the kind of bed a king would be happy to sleep in. He cast his gaze beneath it, and furrowed his brow. "You've remembered something?" I asked hopefully.

"Could it be…?" he murmured. Sir Kenneth shook his head.

"I don't suppose it's inside that…"

"That what?"

"That *box of kisses*," he said, disdainfully.

"Box of kisses?" This mention of a box of kisses rang a bell in my own mind, and its sound sent a shudder through me. "What's inside it?" I asked uneasily. "Not *actual* kisses, surely?"

Sir Kenneth shrugged. "I have always felt it contained *sentiment,* which is why I have never opened it."

I held up a palm. "Say no more. I know better than anyone how sentiment has no part to play in the life of a hero." I approached the bed, knelt down, and pulled out a small wooden box. On its top the word *Kisses* had been engraved. I took it in both hands and shook it gently, as though it might contain an explosive. It did not explode, but rattled. I turned towards Sir Kenneth and extended the box towards him. "Take it and open it," I said.

Sir Kenneth's arms stayed at his sides. "You open it if you must," he said with scorn.

"But this box of kisses is not mine to open."

"You mean you have one too?"

I shook my head. "Of *course* I don't. But if I did have one, which I don't, I would not hesitate to open it. Call yourself a brave knight?"

"That's easy to say when it's not your box." He was right, of course. Sir Kenneth steeled himself. "Hand it over," he said bravely.

A moment later, the lid's box had been tossed to the ground, and Sir Kenneth stared down into it. I say stared, but his eyes were closed and he was muttering something like a prayer under his breath. I peered into the box and smiled, for among the objects within was John's toy soldier. "We've found it!" I whispered.

Sir Kenneth opened his eyes and lifted his chin high, as though knights were impervious to such things as sentiment. But then he looked inside the box again and his eyes grew misty with sorrow. He drew a deep breath, reached into the box, and took out a photograph of two grown-ups.

"Are they your parents?" I asked.

"Yes, I remember now," he said quietly. In the photograph his parents were smiling and waving at him. "Why did they abandon me, Peter?" he asked.

"They didn't."

"Then I abandoned them?"

I squeezed his shoulder and nodded. "But the choice… it was no longer yours to make."

Sir Kenneth furrowed his brow. "Where are my parents?" he asked.

"In the real world, where you left them."

Sir Kenneth's eyes opened wide, as though he'd spotted something of great importance. "Of course! Great Ormond Street. I must get back there. Mother and Father will be worried about me."

"No, they won't. Not anymore."

Sir Kenneth shuddered as he came to the same false conclusion as his parents. "Am I *dead*, Peter?"

I shook my head so hard I might easily have pulled a neck muscle. "Answer me this: do dead children slay dragons?"

"It sounds unlikely. So where *are* we?"

"In the Neverland."

Sir Kenneth looked about him. "Is the Neverland real?"

"It's as real as anywhere else," I confirmed.

"But my parents *think* I'm dead?"

I nodded. "They are lacking in imagination, so what else were they to conclude?"

"They must have grieved for their only son. And yet I had forgotten them. I don't deserve to be missed."

"Maybe so. But you remember them now."

"Yes, but only because you convinced me to open my box of kisses."

"You would have opened it in time. You didn't *want* to forget them. Otherwise why bring these things here?" I reached in and took out John's toy soldier. "And that goes for your good friends the Darlings. You *wanted* to remember them."

"They grieve for me too?"

"Yes, and their gloom is of the most serious kind."

"How serious?"

"So serious that I fear they may grow up before their time."

"Would that really be such a bad thing?"

"The worst. Don't you know? To grow up too soon is the greatest tragedy that can befall anyone. If it happens to the Darlings they will no longer be able to fly, and should that happen they will never be able to visit the Neverland and fulfil their oaths to you."

"Oaths?"

"Yes. To say goodbye."

Sir Kenneth nodded. "I remember now." He took John's soldier from the box and handed it to me. "Then you must take this to them, and without delay."

Journal entry no. 11

With John's toy soldier in my possession, I returned to my own Neverland, but moved swiftly through it on my way to the Darlings.

I arrived in the real world, and found it to be much colder than when last I visited. For this reason their bedroom window was closed. I pressed my nose against the frosty pane and, but for the pink glow that came from the little night lights beside their beds, it was black as pitch inside. I tapped on the window, and tapped again as a chill wind nipped at my sides. I was relieved to see movement within and, moments later, the window was opened. I flew gratefully inside.

"You'll catch your death of cold!" said Wendy, rubbing her shoulders in her night dress. "Have you no coat?" she added, closing the window.

"The sun keeps the Neverland warm all year round."

"Here the sun neglects us every winter," she said.

"You came back!" whispered Michael. "I knew you would. See, John. I told you Peter would come back."

I looked at John, who sat up in bed and rubbed at his eyes.

"Why ever would you doubt it?" I said.

"You said you'd be back tomorrow, Peter," said Wendy.

"And here I am."

"Yes, but it's been two months since your last visit."

Michael rolled his eyes. "John said you were never coming back because you stole Kenneth's knight."

"Stole?" I raised my eyebrows.

"Yes," said John. "What else would you call it? But you're here now, so I presume you've come to give it back." He extended a hand towards me.

I shook my head. "That is not why I'm here."

"See, Wendy. I told you your *friend* was nothing but a common thief," said John.

"Oh, Peter," said Wendy. "What have you to say to that?"

"That I have brought you something to replace it."

"You *can't* replace something like that," said John tearfully. "Not ever. It belonged to my best friend, and I shall never see him again."

"I'll wager that *this* will replace it," I said, extending my hand and uncurling my fingers to reveal his soldier.

John climbed out of bed and took it from my hand. "But it *can't* be the soldier I gave to Kenneth," he said, and moved to his night light to examine it.

73

"Well?" said Wendy.

John gazed at her over his shoulder, his mouth fallen open and his eyes filled with wonder. "It is! It's the soldier I gave to Kenneth."

"And you're sure?" said Wendy.

John nodded. "It has two tiny scratches on its chest from that time when Kenneth and I hurled stones at each other's army." His gaze jumped to me. "The hospital searched everywhere for it. They were *certain* it was lost. So where did you find it?"

Michael took a step towards his brother, and smiled the smile of the knowing. "Isn't it obvious, John? Kenneth must have given it to him."

"He is *Sir* Kenneth now, and he is the bravest knight in Camelot."

"Honestly?" said Michael.

I crossed my heart. "We slew a dragon together." Michael's mouth opened as if to speak, but he made no sound.

The same could not be said for John, who asked, "I'm not saying I believe you. But *if* it were true, if Kenneth is a knight in Camelot, why would he want to know us?"

"I will not lie. When at first I found him he had no memory of his life here, but that is always the way with new arrivals to the Neverland. But those who *wish* to remember in time, are permitted a box of keepsakes. We found Sir Kenneth's box, and your toy soldier had been given pride of place inside it."

74

John looked down at the soldier in his hand. "He didn't want to forget us, then?" he said quietly.

"No. And once his memories were restored, it became his fondest wish that I return the soldier to you."

"Why?" asked Wendy.

"So that you would be unburdened of your heavy hearts, learn to fly, and travel to the Neverland to fulfil your oaths to him."

"To say goodbye?" asked John.

"To say goodbye," I repeated.

"Does this mean that you're going to teach us to fly now, Peter?" asked Michael, finding his voice again. I bowed low and smiled.

The twelve pages that followed here explained everything a person (of sufficient imagination) needs to know in order to fly unaided, but on Tink's advice I have erased those twelve pages. She has been checking my diary, and when she read them she enquired if I'd lost my mind. "Never easy to tell. But why do you ask?" I enquired back.

"Because you can't write down secrets like that where people in the real world can read them."

I folded my arms. "And why not?"

"Because the skies of the real world will end up filled with flying people."

I chewed on a nail. "If you've a point to make, fairy, then make it quickly," I said.

"Perhaps the clue can be found in the word *real*."

I chewed my nail some more. "Flying's real," I said.

"In the Neverland, perhaps. But in the real world they need contraptions with wings and motors to overcome the laws of gravity. There are *physics* in the real world, Peter, and they must be respected."

"Why?"

"I think you'll find that's the whole point of the *real* world."

And so, reader, it is with a heavy heart that we must rejoin the Darlings some thirty minutes later, as that is how long it takes to teach a novice in the real world to ignore the laws of physics and fly. And that novice was called Michael Darling. "Yippee! Look at me, Wendy! John, look! I'm really flying!"

Wendy silently clapped her little brother. "You really believe that I'll be able to do that?"

"It is not for me to believe, Wendy. It is for you. And then nothing can prevent it."

John shook his head slowly. "Nothing but *gravity*," he murmured.

"Simply ignore gravity. And ignore John. Just as Michael is," I told Wendy.

John folded his arms. "Yes, go on then Wendy. Simply ignore gravity as Michael is."

"But I'm not so young as Michael, Peter," said Wendy. "Please explain how to ignore gravity one more time?"

You will know the drill by now… and so we must rejoin the story two pages later (as two pages was what it took to sum up the previous twelve).

"I'm doing it!" cried Wendy.

"Call that flying?" said Michael as he darted about the room.

"If not flying, then what would you call it?" she asked him.

"You're floating," said Michael.

Wendy looked at me imploringly. "You've done the difficult part," I said. "Now all you have to do is *will* yourself to move in the direction you want to go."

She looked up into the top left-hand corner of the room and shot backwards in the opposite direction. I caught her before she flew out of the window. "What happened then?" she asked, strangely content to be held by me.

I put her down. "You may have been looking where you wanted to go, but you must have been thinking about me."

"You know, I believe I was. I was thinking how much I didn't want to let you down."

"That's just it. In order to fly, you mustn't *think* at all. Do you think to walk in a direction?"

"No, of course not."

"It's the same with flying."

Wendy thought about that, and then flew into the corner of the room she wanted to reach. She floated about to face me. "I see what you mean…" And then off she flew in pursuit of

Michael, and the pair chased each other's pyjama tails like children on a funfair ride.

John had been watching his siblings from the corner of his eye. I flew the two metres to his bed and set down at the end of it. "Now it's your turn," I said.

John shook his head. "I can't."

"Nonsense. You were listening to every word I taught them."

"It doesn't matter."

"And what's more, you can see them doing it with your own eyes. Look!"

John jumped off his bed and threw his arms wide. "Just because I can see them doing it doesn't mean I can too!"

"Of course it does," said Michael from the ceiling.

"That's rubbish," said John. "I can watch a surgeon do an operation, but that doesn't mean I can operate myself, does it!"

"That isn't true. You could carry out an operation quite easily," I said.

"Maybe so, but I'd kill my patient."

I leaned closer to him. "What have I told you all about getting bogged down in tiny details?"

"*Killing* the patient is a tiny detail? What land are you *from*?" asked John.

"The Neverland! A place where nobody has ever needed an

operation."

John went red in his face. "Oh, you… you... you…"

"Me thrice *what*?"

"You think you have an answer to everything."

"I do. And if I don't, then Tink will find me an answer."

Wendy landed gracefully beside me. "Who's Tink?"

"A fairy and a loyal friend."

"She sounds wonderful! And she's a real fairy?"

"As real as any other."

"Can we meet her?" said Michael from the ceiling.

"Yes. Of course. But first your brother must learn to fly."

"Why must I? Why don't you just go without me?"

I looked at John. "Kenneth is more your friend than Wendy or Michael's. Is he not your *best* friend?"

"Rub it in, why don't you?"

"It's true, John," said Wendy. "Don't look at Peter like that. He only wants to help."

"Why? What's in this for him?"

I felt the gaze of all three upon me. "I believe that your coming to the Neverland will result in a great adventure for us all."

John huffed. "Adventures involve danger. How much danger can there be in a place called the Neverland that's filled with little fairies?"

I stepped towards him, my voice little more than a whisper. "Not just fairies... there are cold-blooded pirates and savage Indians, and a crocodile so enormous it would not fit inside this room. What's more, after dark, the things that go bump in the night come looking for terrible mischief, and are themselves frightened away come morning by the creatures that stalk children in their dreams."

John gulped.

I lowered my voice further. "Would you like to hear the greatest part of the adventure?"

Behind me Wendy said, "Yes, Peter."

I turned to face her. "No child from the real world has ever set foot in the Neverland. Not a single one since the very beginning of time." I turned slowly on the spot and pointed from one Darling to another. "That means you three shall be the *first* to make the crossing." I drew my sword with a flourish and stepped towards John.

"What are you going to do with that? Cut me?" he said.

"Not *you,* but your doubts about being able to fly!"

What followed here was a page that explained how to cut away any doubts about defying gravity. And so, reader, we now rejoin the story just as John's feet left the ground for the first time...

"This... this... this ...!"

I placed my fisted hands on my hips and enquired, "This is what?"

"Impossible!" said John, smiling despite himself and rising up to bump his head on the ceiling.

Journal entry no. 12

I suppose the journey to the Neverland could be a little scary the first time. The first big hurdle to overcome (I discovered) was this realisation of John's: "We must be flying as high as the dome of St. Paul's Cathedral!" This truth caused much shrieking and covering of eyes – and that was just me – at which point John said a fruity word that made Wendy blush and Michael cover his ears. This word, I have been reliably informed by Tink, has no place in this diary.

Up we flew, higher still, for that is the direction you must fly in to get to the Neverland, and it wasn't long before we entered something that John called the earth's outer atmosphere. From here the planet Earth can be seen as a ball of blue and white. You might imagine that Michael, being the youngest, would have been the most scared, but the opposite was true: his imagination told him that the higher he travelled the more magical and safer things became. Which of course is true.

What gave John the most concern in the outer atmosphere is best summed up by what he said when he arrived: "There is no air for us to breathe in the earth's outer atmosphere! We're all going to die!" He repeated this fiction thirteen times, and only stopped when Michael puffed out his cheeks and blew a raspberry in his face. "See! There's plenty of air to breathe!"

"How is this possible?" said John between gapes.

I flew back to him. "As I taught you, once unlocked, the power of your imagination can make anything possible."

Next came outer space: a void of darkness where the nearest stars are so far away they appear impossible to reach. For a time, my companions were filled with awe as they flew towards billions of stars. John even gave Michael and Wendy the thumbs up, as if to say travelling to the Neverland had been all his idea and what a brilliant idea it had been. But the trouble with those who live in the real world is this: they grow bored quickly, and feelings of awe are replaced by yawns and the desire for something new. And so it was with my companions, whose awe-filled expressions changed to those that said they'd rather be *anywhere* than flying through space towards a galaxy of stars that came no closer. I suppose that's why what happened next caught them unawares. I speak of the secret black hole that is the shortcut to the Neverland. The Neverland lies beyond any star that is visible to the human eye, and so a shortcut is needed to arrive there in a single evening. When at first you fly into the secret black hole, all the stars in the heavens appear to have been snuffed out, and you are blinded by darkness. Soon after that, the quickening begins, and it feels as though you've entered a tunnel where all the stars in the galaxy rush by at astronomical speed. I know to keep my eyes closed during the quickening. This explains why, when I shot out the other side of the black hole over the Neverland, I was able to fly straight and true. And also why my companions fell like shrieking stones into the mermaid's lagoon.

I set down on a rock at the edge of a lagoon beside a mermaid called Miss Roe. "Hello, Peter," she said, flip-flopping her tail against the rock upon which she was sunbathing.

"A good morning to you, Miss Roe," I said.

She gazed out to where my companions were splashing about in the lagoon. "Friends of yours?" she asked.

I nodded. "Indeed. They have just arrived from the real world."

"That doesn't really excuse the dreadful din they're making."

I folded my arms. "Forgive them."

"Why?"

"Because it is the first time that anyone has ever made the crossing from the real world to the Neverland."

"Maybe so, but if they carry on making that *din* they're going to attract the attention of the crocodile. Peter?"

"Yes?"

"Can they swim?"

"Who knows? It never came up." I took a step to the edge of the rock, and placed a hand over my eyes to shield them from the sunlight. "They look to be doing something similar to swimming," I said.

"Splashing about in no particular direction is nothing like swimming. Take it from someone who knows."

"No particular direction? A problem easily rectified," I said, sticking two fingers in my mouth and whistling. They stopped splashing about in no particular direction for a moment, and then began splashing towards the rock upon which I now sat beside Miss Roe.

I have thought long and hard about the word that best sums up how the Darlings looked when they finally climbed out of the water onto the rock. The one I finally chose was this: bedraggled. Panting, they lay on their backs for some time, and John was the first to speak. "He's trying to kill us!" he said, between gasps.

"You said you wanted an adventure," I reminded him.

"Oh, Peter. What if we'd drowned?" said Wendy.

"You can't drown. Not in the Neverland."

"How can you be so sure?" asked Wendy.

"Because nobody ever has."

John struggled up onto his elbows and looked at me. "You think we can breathe? Underwater?"

"You managed to breathe in outer space, didn't you? Correct me if I'm wrong, but isn't there even *less* air in outer space than underwater?" My logic must have been sound, because John nodded and lay back down.

Wendy sat up. "I had no idea the Neverland would be so beautiful!"

"Yes!" said Michael. "It looks just as I imagine Treasure Island to look." He turned and looked at me. "And are there really pirates here?" he said, noticing Miss Roe. At this juncture, it should be recorded for posterity that the spotting of Miss Roe was not Michael Darling's finest hour. He scrambled to his feet as though his pants were set alight and said, "Wendy, John, look! It's a big smelly fish with a pretty face and red hair!"

Wendy and John stood just as quickly, and all three gaped at Miss Roe. The scales on Miss Roe's golden tail bristled. "The flies in the Neverland are as big as fists and carry twice the punch," she accurately informed them.

"Really?" said Michael, gazing about. "What should we do?"

"Close your mouths," said Miss Roe. Three mouths snapped shut.

Wendy was the first to find her manners. She stepped forward and curtseyed. "I'm Wendy Darling," she said, "and I've always wanted to meet a mermaid." Her brothers did the same (with bows that appeared suspiciously like my own) and, once the introductions were done, Wendy insisted they lie beside Miss Roe and sunbathe until their clothes were dry. "I won't have Michael catching his death of cold," she said.

They had not been sunbathing long when Tink arrived. "So here you all are!" she shrieked, appearing in a sudden puff of smoke. So sudden and dramatic was Tink's appearance that everyone present jumped to their feet (including Miss Roe, who has no feet, and a moment later she'd fallen in the lagoon).

"Who *is* this?" asked Wendy.

I was going to tell her who *this* was when *this* spoke for herself. "*I* am Tinker Bell. And who is *this*?" said Tink, looking Wendy up and down.

I gave Wendy a moment to answer, but her expression led me to believe that meeting a fairy for the first time, and discovering her to be so rude, had robbed her of the power of speech.

"Wendy *darling* isn't at all what I was expecting," said Tink.

"You took the words from my mouth," said Wendy.

"How dare you insult me at a time like this?" said Tink.

"Is this a bad time? I had no idea," replied Wendy politely.

"Then you can't have much of an idea about anything, as this is the very worst time," said Tink, clasping her cheeks.

"What's the matter with the fairy lady?" yelped Michael.

Tink fluttered her pretty wings. "Thank you for asking, young man." The young man blushed, and Tink leaned forward so they were eye to eye. "You see," she said, "while Peter was off frolicking in the real world with all you little *darlings*, the pirates attacked the Indian settlement."

Michael clasped his cheeks now. "They did?"

"Yes. They attacked them in the dead of night and took them by surprise. By now they must have wiped out half their number."

"Tink!" I said. "Is that true?"

"Please tell your friend Peter that it is true. And that *that* isn't all."

Michael looked at me. "It is true and that's not all," he said.

"There's more?" I asked.

"Tell Peter that when someone says *that's not all,* it generally implies there's more, yes."

"Tink!" I said.

She straightened up and looked at me. "Hook discovered that one of his clocks was missing, and convinced himself the Indians were responsible."

"But why? I took it."

"It seems that Hook has been looking for an excuse to attack the Indians after dark," said Tink.

"He needed an excuse?" said John.

I thumped my fist into my palm. "It is *the* unwritten rule of the land that both sides agree on a time *and* a place before a battle can commence."

"Hook's broken this rule?" asked Michael.

"So it seems," I said. "For how else was he to win an outright victory against such a brave foe?"

"Why did you steal his clock, Peter?" asked Wendy.

"It was not Hook's clock. He stole it, and I needed it. It contains powerful magic, magic that allowed me to cross into Kenneth's Neverland."

"So this attack on the Indians is our fault," said John.

I glanced at all three Darlings in turn. "Do not trouble yourselves. Only Hook and his bad form are at fault here."

"It's only a matter of time before he slaughters all my kin," came Tiger Lily's tired voice. We looked up to see Tiger Lily standing on a rock above us. Her face was smeared with dirt, and she looked exhausted from battle. "I have run out of arrows," she said, a tear rolling down her cheek.

"You poor beautiful girl!" cried Wendy, reaching up with both arms as though to hug her.

"Where is Chief Hiawatha? Is he safe?" I asked Tiger Lily.

"He's holed up with the other survivors at Moat Creek. But for how long? Hook has them surrounded and hopelessly outnumbered."

"Then we must go to their rescue!"

"*We?*" said Tink. "I trust you don't mean us and these earthly *darlings*."

"Don't you like us?" asked Michael.

Tink glared at Wendy, then smiled sweetly at Michael and said, "You are nice enough, little man., but Peter should never have brought you here. The Neverland is no place for children of the real world."

"Why not?" asked John.

"Haven't you been listening? It's too dangerous," said Tink.

"It's dangerous in the real world, too," John informed her. "Very dangerous. There are wars and fighting there too."

"Maybe so, but none that are fought by *children*," said Tink, folding her arms.

"They're not in the real world now. They're in the

Neverland," I said.

Tink glanced at Wendy again, and fluttered her wings impatiently. "And?" she asked.

"And the Neverland *is* imagination. So there are no limits here, and they can become whatever they want," I said.

"With a little help from me, you mean?"

"Please, Tink," said Tiger Lily. "Do whatever you have to to help my people survive."

Wendy stepped forward. "I want to help. Truly I do."

"Me too," said Michael.

"And me," said John.

"Cock-a-doodle-doo!" I crowed. I took to the air and flew around them so fast as to make them dizzy. I tapped Michael on his shoulder and said, "Which great warrior would you like to become?"

Michael thought for a moment, and then his face lit up. "I learned about Perseus in school recently. Did you know he had winged boots that meant he could fly?"

"He did?" I said.

"Yes! And a golden shield that reflected the gorgon's stare back at her. It turned her to stone. Might I have a shield that can turn *anyone* who stares into it to stone?"

"You shall have your shield! And you will become the Perseus of your imagination! Make it so, Tink."

Tink stamped her foot.

"Impertinent fairy! Make it so or I shall never again call you friend."

Tink poked her tongue out at me, then transformed into a ball of light that darted about Michael's shoulders and sprinkled fairy dust upon them. The dust was absorbed by Michael's imagination, and together they transformed him into the Perseus he'd imagined during his classes. Once Tink had finished, Michael was wearing a bronze breast plate and bronze boots with white feathered wings, and strapped to his arm was a golden shield that could turn any enemy who saw their reflection in it to stone. Michael smiled and took flight on the air of his winged boots. "Do be careful, Michael!" Wendy called up to him.

Next, Tink turned her attention to John. She flew about his shoulders sprinkling her fairy dust. John's eyes lit up. "I shall be the Duke of Wellington!" he said. "The greatest military strategist who ever lived!"

"Are you sure?" I asked.

"Yes, of course. If we're to save the Indians we're going to need the tactical brilliance of a great general."

"Then make it so, Tink!" John was suddenly on a tall black horse, dressed in the gold braided uniform of a general. He drew a long thin sword from a scabbard at the horse's side, and both horse and rider took to the air. I turned to Wendy. "And what will you become?"

Wendy shook her head. "I'm sorry, Peter. I have no heroes of violence as Michael and John do."

"You must *think*, Wendy," I said.

"I suppose I could become Florence Nightingale."

"What weapons did she wield?" I asked.

"She had no weapons. Just bandages and antiseptic. She was a nurse."

"We have no need of bandages in the Neverland."

Wendy looked appalled. "But why ever not?"

"Because in the Neverland, non-fatal wounds heal themselves quickly. There must be someone you've always wanted to be?"

Wendy sat down and thought for a moment. "I want to be the best mother a child ever had one day."

I knelt down beside her. "Then you shall become Mother Nature, and protect the children of Tiger Lily's people."

Wendy smiled at me, and so sweet was her smile that it stole my breath away.

"Yes!" cried Tiger Lily. "Turn Wendy into Mother Nature, and let her protect the children of my people."

Wendy nodded, closed her eyes, and said, "Yes, Peter. Please, make me Mother Nature."

Tink sprinkled her dust on Wendy, and all at once she was dressed in a dark green toga. The toga was made from all the things of the forest that possess life-giving and healing qualities. Wendy opened her eyes and smiled up at her brothers. "I *am* Mother Nature," she said with certainty.

"What powers do you have?" asked Michael.

Wendy held out her hands, and produced a gust of wind that sent Michael laughing and tumbling head over heels. "I imagine I can make thunder and lightning, too!" she said, flying up to join her brothers.

Journal entry no. 13

A little later, we were joined by the Lost Boys. We lay on a high ridge that looked down upon the creek where the Indians had retreated. Tootles, Nibs and Slightly were at the end of our line beside the Darlings in their new guises as heroes. "Are you really Mother Nature?" Tootles whispered to Wendy, who lay beside him.

"Yes. For the time being, anyway."

"Will you be *my* Mother Nature?" pressed Tootles hopefully.

"If you'd like me to be," said Wendy.

Tootles looked very serious. "I speak for all the Lost Boys when I say we'd like that very much."

Nibs inched forwards so he could see past Tootles to Wendy. "It's true," he said. "Tootles does speak for all of us. You see, not one amongst us has ever had a mother. Let alone a Mother Nature."

"Is that why you stare at me so?" asked Wendy.

The Lost Boys nodded.

Tink tutted. "Don't I look after you all?"

The Lost Boys shook their heads.

"That's gratitude for you," snapped Tink. She fluttered her long eyelashes at me and said, "*You* don't look upon me as being a mother, do you, Peter?"

"Of course not, Tink."

Tink smiled and stuck her tongue out at Wendy.

"Would you please stop this bickering!" commanded Tiger Lily.

"Tiger Lily is right. We must concentrate on the adventure at hand," I said.

John was studying the creek below us through a telescope. "It's very quiet," he observed. "The pirates must be waiting till dusk to finish what they started last night."

I scrambled to my feet and drew my sword. "The sun is about to set, so we attack now." I looked to John in his guise as the Duke of Wellington and saluted. "What is your plan, great general?"
John leapt up into the saddle of his horse. "Wendy and Michael, you will distract Hook's men from their left side. Wendy, send powerful winds down upon them, and Michael, when they look to see what has caused these winds, fly down and use your shield to turn any pirate foolish enough to look up into stone."

"It sounds an awfully important job," said Michael.
I saluted both. "And one that you and Wendy are more than up to."

"Peter," said John, "you and the Lost Boys will attack the

advancing pirates from the rear."

"An excellent plan, General. And where will you be?"

"I will stand as a barrier between the pirates and the surviving Indians. If that's alright with you?"

"I defer to your superior knowledge of the battlefield," I said, bowing. "And now we put your plan into action."

The first thing Wendy did was to swoop low over the Indian survivors. She saw many petrified children in the arms of their mothers, and her instincts to protect these children overwhelmed her. Wendy conjured winds so powerful that their like had never been felt in the Neverland before. The pirates were forced to bend double and place their hands over their eyes to shield them from the debris that flew at them. Any pirate who squinted up, curious to see the source of those terrible winds, beheld Michael swooping down upon them, and any who saw their own reflections in his shield were turned instantly to stone. The pirates who witnessed this turned and fled into the avenging blades of Peter Pan and the Lost Boys.

While this was going on, Hook and a handful of his most trusted lieutenants had advanced upon the last surviving Indians. Hook, motivated by blood-lust and villainy, and riding a black steed, soon encountered the only person who now stood between him and victory over the Indians: the Duke of Wellington on his horse. "You will not get past me!" cried John.

"What have we here?" sneered Hook from his saddle. "A little *boy* dressed up like a general?"

"I am the Duke of Wellington, the greatest strategist in the history of warfare!"

"Never heard of you," said Hook.

"Let that be your undoing," said John, his horse rearing up on its hind legs.

"I don't know who you think you are, *boy*, but you do not even belong in this world. Which is why I'm going to slice you in two and send both parts back to where they came from!" Hook galloped forwards. Sword smashed upon hook, and hook upon sword, until John, overpowered by his grown-up foe, tumbled from his mount. Hook climbed down off his horse and stood over his quarry. "Prepare to meet thy doom, *boy*." John raised his sword to deflect the hook that now plunged towards his heart. He tried to stand, but each time he was thrown back down. Hook caught John's sword, which flew from his grasp and left his heart exposed. It was then that another warrior on a horse thundered down upon them both: a knight in silver armour and holding a lance.

"What's this?" said Hook. "Are we to be deluged by interlopers who have no place in our Neverland? Come and taste the deadliest steel in any land, if you dare, little knight!" The little knight *did* dare, and then some. On he came, riding faster and faster, lance held strong and true before him. Seeing that his bluff had been called, Hook thought better of being turned into a pirate shish kebab, and ran for his miserable life.

The knight climbed from his mount and offered his hand to John, who took it without hesitation. He stood up and tried to see the person beyond the eye slits in the knight's helmet. John saw only a pair of dark eyes, gazing back at him, unblinking. The knight lifted off his helmet and cast it to the ground. Two boys stood facing one another, young men who had been the very best of friends until separated by… by what, reader? By what grown-ups lacking in imagination have labelled *death*? John was the first to smile, but only by a fraction. Kenneth extended a hand for him to shake. John ignored it, and instead stepped forwards and threw his arms around his best friend. At first Kenneth froze. As you must doubtless be aware, hugs between boys are not necessarily the done thing.

"I thought I'd never see you again!" said John, with a smile so big that his face struggled to contain it. "And just look at you! You've become the brave knight of legend that you always wanted to be."

Kenneth shook his head. "At this moment it means nothing. I'm just your friend."

John glanced down at the splendid, gold braided uniform he was wearing. "And neither am I the Duke of Wellington." Both boys laughed and shook hands with gusto.

I had been hovering just above them, and now I set myself down. "Our reunion would never have been possible without Peter," said Sir Kenneth.

John offered me his hand. "I'm sorry for doubting you, Peter," he said. I shook his hand warmly.

Wendy and Michael landed beside us. "Kenneth!" cried Wendy. "Is it really you?" She threw her arms around him.

"Hello, Kenneth," said Michael, with no little awe in his voice.

"And hello to you too, young Michael Darling!" said

Kenneth.

"Your armour's amazing," said Michael. "Are you completely safe inside it?"

"Not completely, but I wouldn't recommend taking on a fire-breathing dragon without it."

"How did you get here?" marvelled Wendy. "I thought we'd have to visit another Neverland to find you."

"I am curious to hear the answer to that myself," I said.

Kenneth went to the saddlebag on his horse, opened it and lifted out the clock with four faces. "I discovered this in my land, and sensed there were people beyond it in peril. People I care about. So you see, I had to come."

Journal entry no. 14

After Chief Hiawatha had emerged from the undergrowth and thanked us for saving his people, and Sir Kenneth and I had pointed out that it was all in a day's play for us, Wendy, Michael and I flew to my underground hideout. John and Sir Kenneth raced each other over land on their horses, while the Lost Boys followed on foot. When I arrived back, I drew a finishing line in the sand for John and Sir Kenneth.

The two friends soon came thundering around a rock in the cove and across the finishing line. "A photo finish!" I cried.

Wendy gazed out over the golden beach to the bluest of seas beyond. "Is this really where you live, Peter?" she asked.

I breathed in deeply and filled my lungs with warm sea air. "Yes. Do you like it, Wendy?"

"Very much," she replied. "But where are your things? Do you sleep on the ground?" The Lost Boys had arrived by this time, and all three laughed at her as though she were their real mother.

"No, Wendy," I said. "The entrance to my home is hereabouts."

"Entrance?" said Wendy. "But all I see are trees."

"Could it be that the entrance lies within one?" I said.

"You live inside a *tree*?" asked Wendy.

"Not inside but underneath," I said, glancing at a spot on the ground between two trees. Wendy ran to the spot and examined one of the trees, while Michael ran his fingers over the trunk of the other. He looked across at his sister. "The entrance *must* be in your tree, Wendy," he said.

"I was about to say the same to you, little brother."

"You *both* need to look harder," said Kenneth.

"Oh, we do, do we, clever clogs?" said Wendy. "Over to you," she said, standing aside and beckoning Michael to join her.

Sir Kenneth stood between the two trees and stroked his chin thoughtfully. John joined him and tapped on one of the trees, while Sir Kenneth looked up into its branches. "Would you fly up there and bring me the stick that rests on that branch, old friend?" he asked John.

"I'd be delighted!" replied John, flying up to retrieve the stick. He landed and handed it to Sir Kenneth, who held it diagonally before him. The gnarled stick was over twice his height. Sir Kenneth planted one end of the stick firmly in the ground at his feet.

"Nothing's happening," said Wendy, sounding rather pleased.

Sir Kenneth smiled, lifted the stick onto a horizontal plane, and stepped back so that one end of it went into a groove in the bark of one tree, and the other end did the same in the other. "Open sesame!" I cried, as the sand beneath Sir Kenneth's feet fell inwards as though through an egg timer. Moments later, he was standing at the top of the stairs that led into my underground den.

"Bravo!" cried John, clapping his friend.

Wendy saw that I was looking skyward and that my lips were moving. "Who are you talking to?" she asked.

"I was thanking my lucky stars that Sir Kenneth is not a pirate. If he were, they might have discovered the entrance too, and murdered me while I slept."

"May I be the first to see it?" asked Wendy, making her way to the sand-covered stairs.

I bowed low and beckoned her towards the entrance. "Sir Kenneth, please step aside and allow Wendy Darling to descend into my home."

Sir Kenneth stepped off the top step, and Wendy went down into my den as though it were her own. We all crouched by the entrance to await her verdict.

"It's nice and cosy," came her voice.

"I am glad you find it so," I called down.

"Although, it's obviously a place where a *boy* lives," she said.

The Lost Boys patted my back. "All the better for it!" I said.

"That explains why it needs a woman's touch," came Wendy's reply.

We all shook our heads. "I'd rather you touched nothing," I called down.

"Just a little spring-clean. I promise not to disturb anything," came her busy-sounding voice.

I turned to Tink, who had just fluttered down and joined us. "Tell me, fairy, is it springtime?"

Tink wrinkled up her nose. "Why ever would you ask such a thing? You know it's always summer in the Neverland. What's going on?"

"It's Wendy," said Tootles. "She says it's time that Peter's den had a spring-clean."

Tink clenched her fists, and made to descend the steps. I grabbed hold of her arm. "She's only trying to help. I trust her," I said.

"Oh, you do? Well, be it on your head when she's done *spring-cleaning* and you can't find anything you need."

While Wendy spring-cleaned in perpetual summer, the rest of us played on the beach. We built sand knights and soldiers, and John and Kenneth captained their armies. The battle commenced in earnest, and we hurled sticks at the two opposing sand armies. Before long, all but one sand figure remained – a soldier, which meant John's army had been victorious. I saw how Sir Kenneth had held back towards the end. He had let his friend win. *The very epitome of good form*! I thought.

It was not long after this battle was over and Wendy had re-joined us, that Sir Kenneth said something that caused the hearts of the Darlings to sink. "The time has come for me to return to my own Neverland. Therefore, we must say our goodbyes."

"Must you go so soon?" said Michael.

Sir Kenneth nodded. "The people of Camelot rely on me to protect them."

"What should I tell your mother and father?" said John quietly. "They miss you and grieve for you so much."

Sir Kenneth placed a hand on his shoulder. "Tell them they needn't be sad, that you've seen me, and that I live on, and could not be happier. And be sure to tell them that I love them."

"But what if they don't believe me?" said John.

"They will *want* to believe, and so in time they will come to believe."

"Neverland has made you very wise," said John.

"If it has, it can only mean one thing: that wisdom comes from facing and overcoming our fears."

"More than that," I said, "it comes from looking upon every fear we encounter as nothing more than a new adventure that must be undertaken." I looked at the Darlings, who appeared melancholy despite the wisdom I had shared. "Buck up," I said. "The time has come for you all to fulfil your oaths."

Wendy was the first to hug Sir Kenneth goodbye, followed by Michael, and then by John, whose hug was the most heartfelt of all. Sir Kenneth went to his saddle bag and lifted out the clock with four faces. He set it upon the ground and opened the entrance and the exit. He turned to his friends. "I shall value your friendship always, and never forget you."

"Nor we you," said Wendy, as she was the only one who could find her voice.

"Farewell!" said Sir Kenneth, whereupon horse and rider shrank and galloped through the clock's entrance. The Darlings stared down at the exit, but Sir Kenneth did not reappear. He was already back in his own Neverland. A heavy silence followed, soon broken by Wendy. "I have something to show you, Peter," she said.

"What is it?" I asked. Wendy smiled her sweetest smile, got up and walked down the steps into my underground den. I followed her without thinking, and let that be a warning to all who follow without thinking.

Once below, Wendy went to my bed and retrieved something from beneath it. "Look what I've found," she beamed.

"What is it?"

"It's a little wooden box, Peter."

"You found a *box*?"

"Yes. A box of kisses. Why do you step away from me?"

"Because you are mistaken. That can't be mine. I have no such box."

"Everyone needs kisses, Peter."

"Not I."

"Why not you?" asked Wendy, looking at my lips.

"Need it be said? I am a great hero."

"Sir Kenneth is a great hero, yet he had a box of kisses. So why not you?"

"That's different."

"Why is it?"

"I should have thought it obvious. Sir Kenneth has parents in the real world… people who would miss him." I closed my eyes and turned my head away. "I have no parents, Wendy."

"No parents? Then where did you come from?"

"As with all things in the Neverland, I was born of my own imagination."

When next Wendy spoke, I felt her breath on my ear. "I think you *must* have had parents, and that all you need do is *remember.*" Although chilled to the bone, I felt beads of perspiration on my forehead. *"What's the matter, Peter? You've turned dreadfully pale."*

I opened my eyes. "I *can't.*"

"You can't what?"

"Remember."

"Peter?"

I did not answer her.

"Have you ever seen a single baby in the Neverland?"

"Of course not. The Neverland is much too dangerous for

babies."

"Well, then, haven't you just answered the question?"

"If you've a point to make then make it quickly."

"My point is this: you *must* have been a baby once. And that means you must have been born in the real word, to parents who would have grieved when you went away. You suddenly look so pale and unwell! Turn your back, and I shall put the box back where I found it."

"No! That which is found cannot be unfound. I will open my box. And whatever happens next will just have to be looked upon as all things must."

"And how is that?"

"As an adventure, Wendy."

"Oh, Peter! Your parents would be so proud," she said, handing the box to me.

Journal entry no. 15

I don't remember very much about the journey back to the real world with the Darlings. While not in actual shock, I may have been in a state like it. My ears were ringing, my head felt fuzzy, and my heart was beating too quickly. All had been caused by a single realisation: that I, Peter Pan, *must* have had parents of my own once. Wendy said she'd found the names of my mother and father inside the box. "Leave it in my capable hands, and I will find them for you," she said.

The Darlings had been sitting on their beds when Wendy said it, and John explained that, when it came to finding things, Wendy's hands were by far the most capable. Michael agreed with his brother, and Wendy said I should return in one week's time. "By then I will have found a way to sneak out and visit the public records office," she said. John explained that the public records office was where they kept the records of everyone who has ever lived. I told them I had been alive for a great many years, and that it would not surprise me if the records didn't go back that far.

"Don't be silly," said Wendy. "They've been keeping records since the time of William the Conqueror, and he lived a thousand years ago. I don't think you're as old as all that, Peter."

As I recall, those words were the last that the Darlings and I exchanged before I returned to the Neverland. The week that followed is vague. I recollect being late finding the Lost Boys on four of the seven days, and that on the other three I forgot to find them altogether. Tiger Lily found them, but not until after lunch, by which time they were much vexed. But their vexation was nothing compared to Tink's. What a mood that fairy was in all week long! She had taken to dive-bombing Hook's galleon, and was twice nearly blown to bits by its cannons. "You are a reckless fairy whose luck must soon run out if she's not careful," I warned her.

Tootles raised his hand.

"Yes, Tootles?" I said.

"I seem to remember that in the real world they have something called *anger management*."

"What does that mean?" asked Tink.

"I think it means they teach angry fairies like you how not to get blown to bits by cannons," said Tootles.

"What nonsense!" scoffed Tink. "First of all, they don't have fairies in the real world, and secondly you came here as a small boy. So you couldn't possibly remember something that specific."

"If Wendy does find your parents," said Nibs, "does that mean you'll return to the real world for good?"

Tink folded her arms and looked away from us. "It could mean exactly that," she said quietly.

I shook my head. "She can't *find* them. Not the *actual* them.

Wendy is only looking for a piece of paper. One where a record of my parents is written."

"What kind of record, Peter?" asked Slightly.

"Who could say? Where they lived, or if they had any other children."

"Or when they died, and where they're buried," said Tink hopefully.

"Yes, Tink, exactly. Where they're buried."

Journal entry no. 16

The night I returned to the real world to see Wendy was a peculiar one. First of all, the stars had shifted their viewing positions in the heavens slightly. It was as though they had rearranged themselves to get a better view of something. I hoped it had nothing to do with me, but whenever I glanced in their direction they flickered strangely, as though they they'd been caught in the act of spying. The winds, too, seemed a little out of sorts, and for the entire journey from the Neverland they blew from behind as though trying to hasten me. Even the Darlings's house as I approached it seemed to lean forwards, as if pushing the window closer. I flew through it and discovered the Darlings sitting cross-legged on the floor playing cards.

The children immediately jumped up, and at once my hand was being shaken and my back patted. They stepped aside to reveal a suit of clothes placed on John's bed – a dark suit that lay beside a white shirt and red tie.

"What's this?" I asked.

"It's John's best suit," said Wendy, squeezing my shoulder.

"It's for you to borrow," said John.

"But why?" I asked.

"Because I've found her. I've found your mother, and come first light I'm taking you to see her."

"You've found my mother?" I whispered.

"Yes," said Michael. "And it's respectful to wear a suit when going to visit one's mother for the first time." I had hidden in cemeteries many times, watching young men in their Sunday best visiting the departed.

"Wearing such a garment is a sign of respect?" I asked.

"Yes, Peter," said Wendy. "Now go across the landing into the bathroom with John and he'll help you dress."

"Come on," said John. "I'll help you put on your tie."

We had to be quiet so as not to wake the parents, and when we returned Wendy gasped and placed a hand over her mouth. "What is it?" I asked.

"John's suit fits you so well! You look so handsome, Peter."

At dawn's first light we left through the window and floated to the ground. Wendy stepped off the kerb and took the lead. "We're in the real world now," she said, "and so we're going to behave like real people."

"Meaning?" I asked.

"Meaning we're going to catch a bus."

It was a Sunday morning, and therefore the bus was not packed with grown-ups on their way to make a crust, and before long it pulled up outside the gates of a cemetery.

The gates to the cemetery were open, and we walked through them onto a path surrounded by well-kept lawns. Bluebells grew by the side of this path, and I remembered how people in the real world liked to carry flowers to leave on the graves of the departed. Wendy must be a mind-reader. "Why don't you pick some bluebells for your mother?"

"If you think it a good idea."

"I do."

I picked the bluebells and we continued along the path. Before long I saw a row of gravestones and stepped off the path toward them. Wendy took hold of my arm. "We're not going over there," she said.

"Then where?"

Wendy looked to the path's end, where a grand white building nestled amongst tall trees. When we reached this building, Wendy looked up at its many windows as though she wanted to pick one. She turned to me, centred my tie and said, "Now remember your manners."

"My manners? But why?"

Wendy smiled. "Your mother isn't dead. She lives here, Peter."

I looked up at the building. "You are mistaken. My mother would surely have taken leave of the real world long ago."

"No, Peter. Your mother is very old – one hundred and nine years old, to be exact. Your father departed this world many years ago. I'm sorry, but your mother is still here." Wendy floated up towards the window and reached a hand down to me. "Are you coming?"

I caught her up and looked through the window. Inside, an old woman sat in an armchair beside a bed. She was dressed very smartly, and her cheeks were powdered a bright lilac.

She clutched the top of a cane, and she smiled at its brass top as though it made her happy.

"The window's latch is open, Peter. And she's expecting us," said Wendy.

"She is?"

"Yes. I met with her yesterday and told her to expect a very important visitor."

I pressed my nose to the window. "Is that why she looks so smart?"

"It is."

"Wendy?"

"Yes?"

"Am I the important visitor?"

Wendy smiled at me and nodded.

"Are you sure? I know I am important in the Neverland, but in the real world I am just a phantom, one who visits people in their dreams."

"Not so us lucky Darlings. You came to visit while we were awake, and now you must do the same for your mother. Her name is Lily, and she told me that not a single day has passed when she hasn't thought about you. And that's why she considers you a *very* important visitor." Wendy looked through the window. "Shall we?"

I opened the window and flew inside with Wendy. We landed in the room in front of my mother. She gazed over her cane at me with eyes of the lightest blue that went slowly from top of my head to the tips of my toes. "*Peter!*" she said suddenly.

I nodded and bowed. "Wendy says you are my mother."

Tears welled in her eyes, and she replied with quick nod that said *I am your mother and of that there is no doubt.* Then, with considerable effort, she huddled over the top of her cane and pushed herself to her feet. Once standing, she allowed her cane to clatter to the floor. Slowly, as though balancing on a tight rope, she opened her arms wide.

"Go on, Peter," said Wendy. "Go and embrace your mother."

I took a single step forwards and studied her face. I clasped my hands to my own and pulled the skin back so that my eyes must have been slits. I looked at my mother, and without asking she did the same, rolling back the loose folds of skin until it was pulled taut over her cheekbones. "Yes, I *have* seen you before. I remember now," I said. With a great effort of will, my mother took a step and wrapped her arms around me. I discovered that my mother was stronger than she looked. Much stronger. She clung tightly to my arms and looked into my eyes. "You used to come and visit me in my dreams, Peter. And you looked *exactly* the age you do now."

"I remember," I said uncertainly. "I'm sorry that I forgot to visit you, Mother. I brought you some bluebells."

My mother took the flowers and smiled. "Thank you. Children do forget, but scarcely a day has gone by when I haven't thought about you."

"How did you lose me?"

"You were poorly, and a hundred years ago doctors weren't so good with their medicines as they are today. Where have you been all these long years?"

"The Neverland."

"And you never thought to grow up?"

"Never. Tink would never forgive me if I did."

"Tink?"

"She's a friend."

"Tinker *Bell*?"

"Yes. How did you know?"

My mother asked Wendy to go to her dresser and open the bottom drawer. "You'll see a small wooden box. Bring it to me," she said, her eyes shining with happiness. Wendy opened the box's lid, and my mother reached in and pulled out a brooch. It was a small silver Tink. "I used to wear this brooch when you were a baby… you were fascinated by it and always reached for it."

"Oh my goodness, look at this," said Wendy, taking another object from the box. It was a little red Indian carved from wood. "It's Tiger Lily," she said. "And… oh, look!" she breathed, tilting the box so I could see inside. "There's a pirate with a hook, a pirate's ship, *and* an alligator."

"They were your favourite playthings, Peter," said my mother.

"Why did you keep them?"

"When you visited me in my dreams, you told me to look after them. You said you would come back for them some day." With a shaky hand my mother picked each of the toys out of the box and placed them inside the pockets of John's jacket. "It makes my heart glad that you remember them, Peter."

"Remember them? I have been with them every day since I went away."

My mother was going to say something else but was silenced by the tinkling ball of light that flew in through the window. Tink hovered close to my shoulder and tinkled furiously.

"What is *that*?" asked my mother.

"It's Tinker Bell. Tink, show yourself to my mother." Tink moved to my other shoulder. "It's okay, I give you permission."

My mother placed the back of her hand to her mouth and tears welled in her eyes.

"There is no need to be upset. Fairies aren't supposed to show themselves in the real world," I said.

"Why ever not?" gulped my mother.

"They aren't supposed to exist. Obstinate fairy! Show yourself to my mother!" Tink appeared as her human-fairy self, and looked every bit like the silver brooch my mother had kept.

"Mother meet Tink. Tink, meet my mother."

My mother extended a very shaky hand towards her. Tink glanced at it and raised her chin as though she would not shake it. "Are you going to stay here with your mother?" she asked me.

"Of course not, foolish fairy. I'm only visiting."

"So you'll be returning with me to the Neverland?"

"Of course."

"Alright, then." Tink shook my mother's hand and did a fairy curtsey. "You should know that your son is a great hero in the Neverland," she said.

My mother nodded. "He used to tell me so when he visited me in my dreams."

"Then you'll also know that your son isn't exactly known for his humility."

"I had wondered," she replied.

Tink's expression changed, and she looked at me imploringly.

"What's the matter?" I asked.

"It's Hook. I've never known him so angry as he is over what happened at Indian Creek. He's on the warpath, Peter. He's searching the lagoon, and it's only a matter of time before he finds the Lost Boys."

My mother reached out and cupped the side of my face in her palm. "It sounds as though you're needed, my dear lost Peter. I'm so proud of you."

I placed a hand over my mother's, and smiled reassuringly. Withdrawing my hand, I removed John's suit and tie to reveal my own suit of clothes beneath it. "Please don't be sad, Mother. I promise to come back and see you." I took the toys she had given me from the pockets of John's jacket and, as I handed them to Tink for safe-keeping, my mother watched me intently in case I should drop one.

"I am very old, Peter," she said. "So when you return I may not be here." I placed both my hands on her shoulders. "You must not be afraid, Mother. To leave the real world, even as a grown-up, will be an awfully big adventure."

Tink transformed into a ball of light, flew to the window, and tinkled furiously. "I am coming," I said.

Wendy grabbed my arm. "You will come back and visit us, won't you? John and Michael would be awfully sad if you didn't."

"Won't you be sad, Wendy?"

"Of course I will, you beautiful foolish boy. I shall be the saddest of all!" she said, kissing my cheek.

I placed my hand on the spot. "We shall see," I said. "And now I must go and find the Lost Boys before Hook does!" I flew out of the window, came back, waved one last time, then fixed my gaze on the third star on the left, and flew straight on till morning.

The end

Thank you for reading! If you enjoyed *I Am Pan*, you might also enjoy *Diary of a Wizard Kid 1 & 2* by the same author. The opening pages of which follow here.

Diary of a Wizard Kid

Okay. I know what you must be thinking. But I'm not *that* guy. My name doesn't even rhyme with rotter. It's Jimmy Drummer. And all I've got in common with that guy is we're both wizards. I mean, I didn't even want to be a wizard. Anyway, I got to thinking, there must be a world of kids out there who think going to wizard school over in England would be super cool. Well, if you're one of those kids, I've got three words for you right off the bat: 'pointy hat' and 'broomstick'. You ever caught a reflection of yourself sweeping a classroom in a pointy hat? It's no joke I can tell you. You *still* think being a wizard would be cool? Well, stick around because you haven't heard nothing yet. No word of a lie, you're about to experience the craziest adventure a regular dude has EVER had ...

Wednesday (the day it all happened)

So like I was saying, I was just your average 11-year-old
dude. Which is all I ever wanted to be (until I turned 12).
But, oh no! That was, like, *too much* to ask. Man, it's not
like I even *believed* in dumb magic. Anyway, I was in the
mall recently. Just mooching about. Sucking on a popsicle.
Minding my own. When I noticed this strange dude
wearing a top hat and leaning on an umbrella. He looked
like Mary Poppins's brother or something. Then the dude
winked at me. You heard me right. *Winked.* Man, I tried
real hard not to look at him. But you probably know what
it's like when you try not to look at someone – the more
you try the more you stare right at them. And that's when
he tapped the end of his nose like we shared a big secret. I
figured this was a pretty serious situation. So I slid off my
stool and made a bee line for the exit. And *that's* when my
world changed forever. The guy started swinging his
umbrella and everyone, and I mean *everyone*, got frozen
where they stood. "What ho, young man!" he said, in the
happiest, dumbest English accent you've ever heard in your
whole life. I bet you're thinking that if you found yourself
in a situation like that you'd be all cool about it. Maybe say
something like, 'Oh, hey there English dude! Neat trick
swinging your umbrella and turning everyone in the mall
into mannequins.' Well, I've got news for you: there's *no
way* you would have said that. You'd have yelled
something like, "This SHOULD NOT be happening to a
regular dude!" just like I did. So anyway, the guy started to
twirl his moustache (did I mention he had a moustache?
Well he did. And it curled up at each end.) So he's twirling
his moustache with one hand and swinging his umbrella
with the other when he said, "No need to look so alarmed,

old bean." That's right. He called me an 'old bean.' Then he swung the pointy end of his umbrella right into my knee. Okay, it was an accident. I know that now. The dude is just seriously accident prone. But at the time I didn't know that. How could I? I thought maybe he was crazy enough to think I *was* an old bean. And maybe he hated old beans and went travelling through space and time attacking them with his umbrella. So I told him, "I'm not old, mister! And do I *look* like a vegetable to you? Seriously, dude!" Anyway, I wanted to make a run for it but I couldn't 'cos my knee was killing me. So I made a hop for it. And no word of a lie, he hopped right alongside me. "Now listen here," he said, "I've got something jolly important to tell you."

"Go away!" I told him.

"You're a little confused I can tell. But I can explain it all in a jiffy."

"You deaf or something? Go away! You got the wrong guy!"

"You are Jimmy Drummer are you not?"

"Yeah. No! Whatever! Just leave me alone, dude!"

"I'm afraid I can't. Not if you're Jimmy Drummer of 6 Little Hamlet Street, Ft Myers, Florida, USA."

"How'd you find out where I live?!"

"It's my job to know all about you. What I don't know about you Jimmy Drummer of 6 Little Hamlet Street, Ft Myers, Florida, could fit on the back of a postage stamp."

"You need help, mister! You really do!" That's when he froze me mid hop. So I'm suspended like a foot off the ground. And the only things I could move were my lips. I found that out when I mumbled, "Now this here should *defo* not be happening to a regular dude."

"You, regular? Stuff and nonsense," he said. "You're about as far from regular as a four-headed toad shopping for a toaster at a garage sale. Or a cat with eleven lives and eight legs dancing a tango with a purple rhinoceros. In fact, it could be said that you're about as regular as ..."

"Okay," I mumbled. "Stop with the dumb comparisons. I get it. I'm a freak. Just unfreeze me already."

If you enjoyed this sample, Diary of a Wizard Kid 1 & 2 is available from Amazon.

Made in the USA
Middletown, DE
29 June 2017